Last Stop, Ground Floor

by

David Wilson

ISBN: 979-8-218-21055-7

DEDICATION

To all of law enforcement officers who work so very hard only
to have those deemed guilty of committing crimes receive
punishments far less than what they truly deserve.

And to the victims of those crimes.

CONTENTS

Introduction

On January 29, 1979, a young girl by the name of Brenda Spencer decided that she was bored and opened fire at an elementary school in San Diego, California.

Coincidentally, she lived directly across the street from the school. In the early morning hours, as children and staff were arriving at school, Spencer fired 36 rounds over the course of 20 minutes with a .22 caliber rifle that her father purchased for her, along with 500 rounds of ammunition.

Two adults were killed while attempting to save the children. Eight children were injured, and one police officer also suffered wounds.

After barricading herself inside her home for several hours, and threatening during negotiations to, "Come out shooting," Spencer finally surrendered after authorities promised to buy her a meal at Burger King.

Spencer was quoted as saying that the reason for committing the shooting was, "I don't like Mondays, this was a way to cheer up the day."

Brenda Spencer was a drug and alcohol abuser, by choice. She was 16 years old at the time of the shooting.

The Cleveland Elementary School shooting was the first well-documented school shooting in America. Since this occurrence, there have been thousands of mass shootings in this country alone. In the 2000s, over 80 of the total mass shootings in America were committed in schools. As of August of 2023, in this year alone, over 466 mass shootings have taken place somewhere in the U.S. which includes over 545 people being killed and nearly 1,900 injured. The lives of the survivors, and the lives of the families, are forever changed due to inexcusable violence.

As of September 2023, Brenda Spencer remains in prison, having been denied parole many times. And that's exactly where she should be…until it's her turn.

Part 1

Nick's Arrival

When the elevator doors opened Nick found himself staring at the interior panel that indicated only the three choices; up, down, and a floor in between simply marked as 'P'. As he gazed, he noticed the 'down' button's light go dark, indicating the arrival on the ground floor. He glared more intently and felt that possibly there were no buttons to press. Only tiny, circular lights were next to the three choices to reflect which floor the elevator's destination was to be. Although in his state of perplex, he just wasn't certain.

Nick had yet to notice that he'd arrived on the lower level, or that the elevator doors had even opened. He was all too focused on his thoughts that weren't clear and more than a bit confused. As he continued to stare at the panel, he wondered how he'd come to be in the elevator to begin with, or how long the ride had been. Additionally, how the choice of direction had seemingly been made for him in advance, as he didn't recall pushing any of the buttons, again, if there were any to be chosen. He turned around, finding that the elevator compartment was like any other. Shiny, steel construction with padding on the walls and a wooden rail along the center. The fabric on the padding was neutral off-white in color. It was clean, and bright inside the elevator with some type of light illuminating down from the ceiling. It was also comfortable, as if temperature controlled to a cool 65 degrees.

The young man looked down upon himself and also noticed that rather than the prison-issue, dull gray coveralls with his identification number embroidered where the right-hand pocket should be, he was now wearing his more familiar brown corduroys and a white, short-sleeved T-shirt. The canvas loafers that he recalled being on his feet were now replaced with familiar high-top leather sneakers. All the normal clothing he'd worn daily prior to his incarceration when he was a free man, rather than the prisoner to the justice system he'd been for the past seven years.

Nick also noticed that he had his thick, coke-bottle glasses resting back on his nose that had been taken from him before entering the death room. He removed them to briefly inspect the lenses. He noticed that they were the same ones he preferred that had been broken long ago by another inmate and not the cheap set that the prison eye doctor had ordered which caused his eyesight to be fuzzy. He put them back on and stared down at the panel again, satisfied that they were once again the ones with the prisms that helped keep his eyes from crossing so badly when he stared at things up close.

Nick glanced up when the person standing in the hallway on the other side of the doors cleared his throat.

The man standing before Nick was tall and blond. He appeared to be in his mid-30s and dressed in a nice pink, long-sleeved dress shirt and newer-looking jeans. He was very tidy in appearance. The man was smiling down at Nick, as he was a bit taller. The younger Nick, now only 25 years of age, looked the stranger up and down. He took note that the man's hair was neatly cut, combed, and that he had a bit of facial hair, maybe a day or two's growth. It looked natural on him, though. He also wore large-rimmed glasses. The lenses were not as thick as Nick's, but they were darker as if to be light-sensitive, and his eyes smiled down at Nick as he looked through them.

"Welcome. You may call me Jeffrey."

"Where am I?"

"Oh, come now. You know where you are." The answer came with a bit of sarcasm and a smirk. When Jeffrey spoke, his voice hinted a bit of arrogance, and his natural smile was his trademark.

Nick poked his head out and tilted his body to get a look around behind the polite gentleman. All he could see was a seemingly dark, endless corridor. Nick squinted behind his glasses as he couldn't make out any doorways or intersecting hallways in the distance. The walls beyond the elevator, which appeared to be made up of aging, dark-stained, and burnt-style wooden boards, seemed tight. At the end of each thick, hand-cut, and badly cracked board the rusted nail heads stained the wood where the moisture had seeped and left a trail, further reflecting the age of the construction. Nick looked up, the ceiling disappeared in the darkness above the wide, rough-cut rafters crossing overhead that were held together with rusted plates of steel and bolts.

Nick's immediate thoughts were that it reminded him of the crew's bilge in an old pirate ship from movies he'd watched. He continued to squint, noticing that from the rafters, about every eight feet there extended chains attached to wooden and rusted metal wagon-wheel chandeliers, each containing many hundreds of candles with the light from their flames glowing against the dank walls. The candles were all burnt down, and the melted wax covered the wood. Nick glanced down to see the floors were made from the same ancient lumber that the walls appeared to be, however, it seemed as if none of the wax that was dripping from the chandeliers was striking the floor, or even falling at all. The corridor felt more like a dungeon than anything else to the young man.

As Nick leaned out from the elevator's doors, he felt a

warmth strike him in the face. A warmth that the temperature-controlled elevator had been hiding. It wasn't exactly hot, but it also wasn't comfortable, as if someone had the thermostat turned up far too high.

"Why don't you step out of that elevator and join me? Others are certainly waiting to use it." Nick glanced up, as his barely five-foot, four-inch, and skinny build was being dwarfed by Jeffrey's six-foot-one, semi-athletic stature. Jeffrey smiled down at Nick and signaled him to exit the elevator with a wink and cocking of his head.

Nick cautiously stepped away from the elevator as a cat might enter a room when it suspected another to be waiting to pounce from the other side of the door. He glanced to his left and right as a slight feeling of claustrophobia overtook him. From side-to-side the walls were only about eight feet wide. With caution, he gently stepped out.

Once Nick fully exited into the corridor, Jeffrey placed an arm around his shoulders and turned to face the never-ending cavernous hallway to view it along with the younger man. "There, you see? Nothing to be afraid of. Not yet, at least." The latter statement was emitted with a chortle as he turned to face the young man, "Now, tell me, Nicholas, do you remember anything?"

Nick gazed down the dark and endless corridor, still not having the ability to see an end to it as he responded quietly, "Remember anything?"

"Yes, of course. Do you recall how you came to be in the elevator? Do you remember the ride down? Do you remember anything? What's your last memory?" Jeffrey and the young lad began to walk away from the elevator's doors as they closed behind the two, with Jeffrey having initiated the movement.

Nick looked up and to the right as he formulated the question in his mind while stepping forward with his host. "I remember laying on the gurney." He gazed forward and squinted from behind his glasses, "And I remember turning my head to see the clear liquid and bubbles traveling down the tubes and into my arm." Nick looked up at Jeffrey and squinted again, "I don't remember anything after that."

"Ah, yes. That's about as far as most recall with that sort of thing. Don't worry, it's quite typical as a matter of fact. I'm certain your memory will improve as soon as the effects of the drugs wear off completely." Jeffrey nodded his head slightly as they walked, his arm still around Nick's shoulders and he chuckled, "Do you recall the remark you made to that mother while you were laying there just before the signal for the executioner to begin?"

A confused Nick glanced up, "Remark?"

"Yes, of course. A terrible choice, if you ask me." Jeffrey looked straight ahead with a stern expression. "For the life of me, I don't understand why people hesitate to put more thought into their last words and choose them a bit more wisely." He stopped and faced Nick, holding his free hand palm up with the other remaining on Nick's shoulder. "I mean, your type's goals are always to be remembered, right? You wanted the fame that felt would accompany your crime. Or so, the fame you thought you'd have. I don't understand why people like you choose to say something foolish and nasty instead of thinking for a moment and uttering something prophetic. You know, try saying something sibylline for once. Certainly, something other than the garbage you uttered." Jeffrey waved his hand in front of himself, puffed his chest, and boasted, "At the very least quote someone famous, for goodness sake, if you can't come up with anything on your own. Say something people will remember. That's the point, isn't it?"

Jeffrey turned forward again and they continued strolling, "But no, it's always something hurtful to people who you've already irrevocably damaged. Entirely unapologetic." He looked down, "Either that or your kind utters the pathetic apologies. I truly despise that. It's so weak and insincere. Nobody believes you when you say that you're sorry in the end."

Nick simply stared up at his host, confused to say the

least, and only paying attention to half of what Jeffrey was saying as he unconsciously allowed himself to be guided along.

Jeffrey stopped the two again, "I mean, really. Those were your last words, and you wasted the opportunity entirely." He poked Nick gently in the chest with his free hand and spoke sternly, "And you have no idea how lucky you were that you knew when your final breath was to be taken. You had time to prepare. You had time to give a proper speech. But instead, you ruined it."

They began to walk again with Nick looking back through his thick glasses. With only a few steps, the elevator doors now seemed miles away and fading into the darkness of the candlelight.

Jeffrey continued, "As for myself, like many others, I was robbed of that benefit." Jeffrey's pompous tone and grin returned, "I mean, my day was on the schedule. That is until that pathetic justice system overturned the decision and I was given life instead of death." He chuckled again, "Life. What a concept, don't you think?" Jeffrey shook his head and continued, "But even then, I was still somewhat in control, now wasn't I?"

Nick felt that his host was talking far too much, and he didn't really care what the man had to say other than to explain where he was, and why.

Jeffrey's voice then hinted a bit of anger, "Until that schizophrenic idiot took it all away from me so suddenly while we were in the showers." He regained focus, fluttered his eyes, and cocked his head, "It was my fault, I admit that. I let my guard down. I should have seen it coming. Oh well, at least I was able to provide a good speech at my sentencing hearing." He looked down and winked, "It was perfect, I tell you. I came up with it myself and practiced for weeks. It was a speech to end all speeches." Their eyes met through their glasses before Jeffrey looked back straight. "But, I digress. I mean, this isn't about me today, now is it? Today is all about you, Nicholas."

Nick shook his shoulders as the two strolled, attempting to free himself from the arm holding onto him. Anger and confusion could be detected in his voice. "I don't understand. What's going on? What's going to happen to me? Where are we going?"

"To your room, of course. Your special place. Just yours, single occupancy, no others. We all have our own space here, small as it may be. Yours is quite a distance away, providing us plenty of opportunity for us to go over the rules."

Nick stepped in front of Jeffrey, faced his host by looking up, and spoke sternly, "Wait a minute! What's going on here?! Rules?! Rules for what? Where am I, anyway?! I don't understand any of this!"

Jeffrey spoke calmly with an expression of amusement towards the young lad, "What's there to understand?"

"Where in the hell am I?!"

A surprised look came over Jeffrey's face and he placed a finger to his lips, his eyes darting both left and right from behind his glasses. "Oh, dear. We don't use formal names like that down here. You must be careful not to do that." His expression eased again and he spoke with direction, "Now, look here, this is as good of a time as any to go over the basic rules so you don't get yourself into more trouble than you already are. And yes, there are rules down here. You see, this place is generally what you make of it." Jeffrey shook his head, correcting himself, "What I mean by that is that you will certainly be punished, there's no question. I mean, that's what it's all about, now isn't it? And, it will be quite unbearably painful." He pointed, "But, how you conduct yourself will determine whether that punishment escalates. And, it certainly will escalate, that much is quite inevitable. I haven't seen anyone yet whose punishment didn't get worse than when they started."

The two began to walk again with Jeffrey leading. "Think of it this way. There's your initial punishment that the Boss has created for you…"

"The Boss?"

"Don't interrupt, it's rude." Jeffrey never glanced down as he spoke, "And yes, the Boss. Remember, we don't use formal names down here. It's simply not allowed. We don't ever refer to the Boss by his actual name or formal title. And, certainly no formal references to the man upstairs, either." Jeffrey pointed up with his free hand. "Never, ever mention his name. The Boss doesn't like that at all. Additionally, we also never mention the proper names for the top or bottom floors, for any reason." Jeffrey frowned, "Now, where was I going with this? Oh, yes, punishment. You see, Nick, if you break the rules, such as what I just mentioned, your punishment will become worse. In some cases, much worse."

"I still don't understand."

"Oh, come on." Jeffrey's eyes rolled along with his head, "Work with me here. Don't pretend to be stupid. I mean, you are here for your punishment, aren't you? You must realize that by now, don't you? Why else would you be in the third dimension? You didn't expect this to be a cakewalk, did you?" Jeffrey pointed down, "Now, listen up. You will suffer, and greatly. But just how much over time is up to you."

The two ceased walking again and Jeffrey faced his student, looking down and shaking his head, "And, that's another thing. Time doesn't exist here. Time has no meaning anymore. There are no years, no hours, no minutes. Not even seconds. Only the now." Jeffrey's smile widened, "I mean, you are here for eternity, now aren't you? What use would time serve for you now?" Jeffrey let out a laugh as he continued, "But then, how long could eternity possibly be?"

"I still don't under…"

"To continue," Jeffrey interrupted and began to lead Nick further away from the elevator. "There's your chosen, or should I say, the punishment that has been created specifically for you by the Boss. However, if you break a rule your punishment will be enhanced. Greatly, I'm afraid."

"Enhanced?"

"Yes." Stating proudly, "Quite creatively too, I might add. I mean, you didn't exactly play by the rules when you were alive, now did you, Nicholas? And, your punishment in life certainly didn't fit the crime you committed. So, breaking the rules down here will come with intensely irreversible consequences."

Nick was snarky, "What do you mean by irreversible?"

"Yes, indeed, irreversible. This isn't like solitary confinement, which has a beginning and an ending. Down here there's only a starting point to your punishment with no ending as to how much worse it can become."

"What kind of punishment are you talking about?" Nick's tone remained foul, "Are they based on my crimes?"

Jeffrey chortled, "Oh, come now. That's a bit boring, isn't it? I mean, I suppose it might have a hint of your actions within it somewhere. But, what if everyone's punishment were simply an eye for an eye or a tooth for a tooth? Everyone would know in advance what's coming to them, now wouldn't they? Where's the mystery in that? No, he's far more creative. And, to be fair to you, the punishment will be the same every time. That is to say unless you break a rule and it's enhanced. However, you'll always know how it will start, just not always how it will end."

"End? And, what do you mean by the same thing every time?" Nick's questions annoyed Jeffrey just slightly, as they were presented with sarcasm rather than inquisitiveness.

"Ah, that word again. Time. My apologies. Please, let me explain. Everyone's punishment, or rather, their pain, arrives every so often. On a regular basis, I suppose it's safer to say without the reference to time. Not that I'm attempting to insult Aristotle or anything, but there is a before, a during, and an after. You see, there's a lot of people down here, Nick. That's a lot of punishments to dish out. And, the Boss doesn't necessarily want your punishment to be an ongoing, everlasting event."

The two strolled along with Jeffrey continuing his explanation, "He feels it much more meaningful if it arrives on a cycle. He also feels that the anticipation of knowing what's to come is as brutal as the physical punishment itself. Not to mention, the intensity of the pain is so much worse if you don't know exactly when it will arrive again. You see, Nick, the mind is a wonderful tool for creating intensity and pain in itself, even without the actual, physical pain having begun." Jeffrey pointed again and boasted, "So, not to keep referencing physics, but, to help you better understand, your pain will come and go on a cycle. You will suffer greatly on a regular basis which will certainly include the mental anguish that goes along with the anticipation of not knowing when your pain will return. It's all quite clever, don't you think?" Jeffrey looked down to only a half-attentive and still bewildered Nick. With an evil little gaze and grin forming his host inquired, "Do you understand?"

"Okay, yeah, I guess. But when will mine begin? My pain, I mean?" Nick was losing even more interest in the conversation, distracted by his surroundings as he stared at the walls as they walked along. He felt invisible eyes upon himself through the cracks and crevices in the planking. As if many, many people were staring through them, silently watching the two pass by. He also felt as if they weren't alone in the corridors, although no one else could be seen. It was a feeling that Nick didn't like.

"Don't be in so much of a hurry. Your punishment will come. And don't worry, you won't enjoy it. In fact, you should try to make the best of the brief amount of time that we have together. It will be the last time that you never feel pain." Jeffrey shook his head again, "Oops, sorry. My apologies. I didn't mean to reference time again."

Nick looked away from the walls and hugged himself, rubbing his own arms. Goosebumps had formed and he found himself shivering in the warmth. "I don't get it. Why are you telling me all this?"

"To prepare you, of course. As I said, mental anguish is

just as important as physical. It's so much worse when you realize what's to come, or haven't you figured that out yet? I'm here to guide you to your space and prepare you for what pain is to come. I'm also here to answer questions you may have. Don't worry, you'll have an ample amount of…well you know…to worry about just when it will begin."

Jeffrey looked down at the young man, "It's all part of a plan, and quite amusing to him." Jeffrey perked up, "Oh, and once you arrive, you'll have the opportunity, just once, to see what will happen to you. Sort of like a movie without the popcorn, or comfortable chair to watch it from. He will show you what's to come, and you'll see it happening to yourself. It's like a preview."

Jeffrey glanced down again as they strolled, "So, try to pay attention during our little walk. Again, we need to go over all the rules so you can't say that you weren't warned in advance. The Boss wants to give you every opportunity to do something you couldn't seem to do while you were alive."

Sarcastically, Nick inquired, "And, what would that be?"

"Play by the rules, of course." Staring straight ahead, a big smile crossed Jeffrey's lips as he made the remark.

"Okay, fine." It was apparent in his tone that Nick was quite disgusted with the conversation thus far. "What's this space of mine that you keep mentioning?"

"Your room, of course. I told you already. We all have one. It's where you'll spend your eternity. A place to wait for your pain to come and go, and come again. A tiny, little space where you'll simply sit and wait, and suffer."

"Sit and wait? Just sit? Nothing else?"

"Well, certainly. I told you already, the mental pain and exhaustion are just as important as the physical pain. You'll sit and wait. And wait, and wait until it finally comes around again. Once it has come and gone, you'll begin to wait again for the next time." Jeffrey shook his head, "Oh, darn, I used that word again." He winked and corrected himself as they strolled along, "I really must stop doing that. I don't want to give you the misconception that there's any form of calculated sequence to your existence here."

As the two kept a slow and steady pace Nick found himself looking even more closely at his surroundings, still only half-heartedly listening to anything that was being told to him by his host. He looked at the finer details in the walls as they went by, continuing to feel as if he were being watched. Each of the boards that made up the walls certainly did appear burnt. They also were knotted, cracked, and many bowing out on the ends where they were nailed to whatever framing was behind, another sign of their age. There appeared to be scratching on many of the planks as if someone with long fingernails had fought against being dragged down the corridors. He looked up, the dark-stained rough-cut wooden rafters were at least ten feet high. He still couldn't make out the ceilings, as the light from the chandeliers only seemed to reflect down. He stared at his feet as they shuffled along, the decking below seemed to have a glow coming from beneath and through the cracks as if the entire structure were some sort of suspended catwalk with fires burning underneath it. Only, there seemed no additional heat other than the uncomfortable warmth that surrounded him in the stale air of the space they were in. The floorboards also appeared to be claw damaged, as if many dogs with sharp paws roamed these halls. Each step caused the wood to creak and at times Nick felt as if the corridor were gently swaying, making him feel again as if they were in the bowels of an ancient Viking longship on fire from a cannon shot to the bow below the water line and rocking from the impact and waves. It was causing him a touch of nausea.

The overall odor surrounding Nick was musty, with a sickly hint of leather and tobacco. Overall, the corridor had an eerie, surreal feeling to it. In fact, to Nicholas, with all of the chandeliers ahead appearing the same and progressively darker in the distance, it was similar to gazing into an infinity mirror. It was all tight, dark, and dank. Nick's feeling of discomfort was worsening with each step.

Nick's tone remained sarcastic as he spoke again, not having heard anything just prior to his interruption, "So, how do you know when the pain will happen again? Is there a clock on the wall?"

"You aren't paying attention, are you? What have I told you about quantifying durations here? Time is of no matter. There are no mechanisms for the passage of cause and effect. No bells that will toll on the hours. No second hands to reflect another minute gone by." Jeffrey remained monotone, "So, to answer your question, I'm not certain how it works for anybody. I suppose it's different for everyone. And, for some, it comes with no warning. For others, like me, there are signals reflecting its arrival."

"Signals?"

"Hints, if you prefer. Myself, for example. The screaming of those receiving their punishments just before mine becomes louder when my pain is drawing nearer. When the screaming is such that I can't hear myself thinking clearly, I know it's going to happen soon."

"So, why do you get a warning? I would think it would be more punishing if it just hit you all of a sudden?"

"I don't know." A puzzled expression crossed Jeffrey's face and his tone became snarky, "Maybe he likes me more or something, and provides me with a clue. Who knows? It's not for me, or you, to decide. You don't make up the rules, Nick. You never did. You just never realized that, and tried to make up your own rules regardless."

Nick stopped dead in his tracks and faced his host, his expression and tone turning to even greater anger with his confusion boiling over. "Enough, already! This is all some kind of bullshit!" Nick pointed down the dark corridor, "You actually want me to believe that you're leading me to a tiny room somewhere where I just sit for all eternity and wait for some type of punishment that comes around when the clock strikes midnight?! That's some kind of crap!" Nick stretched both of his arms out in front of himself, "We're in a fuckin' hallway that goes nowhere! I'm supposed to believe that I have a room somewhere at the end of this tunnel where I just sit and wait?!" Nick turned his body around and motioned in all directions. "There's no goddam rooms anywhere down here that I've even seen so far! Where in the hell is everyone?! There's literally nobody here but you and me! Isn't this place supposed to be full of assholes like me?!"

Jeffrey remained calm, adjusted his glasses, and blinked slowly behind the darkened lenses. "Oh, dear. That anger thing. It's so typical for those who commit your type of crime, now isn't it? You really must be careful. You aren't starting well at all." Jeffrey put a hand back on Nick's shoulder and attempted to guide him again. "You've already taken the risk of increasing your punishment with just a few poorly chosen words and we haven't even barely begun our walk together. How do you think you're going to survive eternity doing foolish things like that? He's not going to give you any more free passes, Nick. You've used them all up. So please, I implore you, watch your words."

Jeffrey sighed deeply, "Oh, well, I suppose that's why this walk is so important. Think of it not just as a chance to ask questions, but also as a warning. You really do need to pay attention, Nick. I'm here to prepare you, but you must pay attention and trust in what I say. After we arrive at your destination, there's no more help coming. No more answers to any questions you may have. Just you alone to deal with your thoughts and pain for the duration of your stay. Which, by the way, is forever."

"You want me to pay attention?!" Nick's anger and sarcasm remained, "Pay attention to what?! What is my punishment?! Enough of this! I want to know right now!" Nick had stopped walking again and was frowning angrily up at his host, and he childishly stomped a foot. "Tell me right now!"

"There you go again, being in a hurry and all, and

allowing your anger to get the better of you." Jeffrey's eyebrows raised above the rim of his glasses, "Just like you did before when you went into that school, isn't that correct, Nicholas? And, look where that got you. Where did you end up with your poor decision-making? On the cover of People Magazine? Or Time, or Newsweek? No, right here, that's where." Jeffrey pointed and frowned, "And, I'm telling you right now, once we arrive you'll wish you were still on this little walk of ours together. So, pay attention."

Jeffrey calmly began their stroll again with Nick reluctantly allowing himself to be guided. "Now, to answer your inquiry, as for your pain, it's different for everyone. Think of it as a sliding scale. The worse your sins, or poor decision making if you prefer that over the latter, the worse your initial punishment was to be. So, if you think of what you did in relation to someone the likes of Ivan the Terrible, let's just say, you may just start out fairly easy. I mean, you're really nothing in comparison to someone like that, now are you? In fact, you're pretty much nothing in comparison to anyone."

Jeff's arrogant chuckle found its mark in the statement as Nick threw him a dirty glance.

Jeffrey continued, "It's all relevant, though...I mean, if you truly think about it. If you continually break the rules down here your punishment can become so much more intense than others who started out worse off than you did. The difference being, they made the smart choices to play by the rules. But then again, who's to say whose punishment is worse? Maybe your punishment will be just as bad as it is for Kim Jong-un, or possibly Stalin. It's all up to the Boss in the end, or the beginning if you prefer, now isn't it?"

Nick stared blankly for a moment as they walked together, his frustration and confusion still on edge. He forced himself to calm down, truly having more questions he wanted answered. "Okay, fine. Tell me more about how to break the rules. And, where is everyone? There are no rooms anywhere in here. Where are all the ones from before me?"

Jeffrey threw him a befuddled glance as they walked together. "I'm not sure what you mean, Nick. There's a room right here."

Part 2

The Student and the Teacher

Jeffrey motioned to his immediate right and there appeared a door. A door that Nick either hadn't noticed or that hadn't been there just moments earlier. The door, constructed with the same timeworn lumber, was recessed into a frame that was rounded at the top, nearly seven feet high at the peak. A large, wooden handle was wrapped in heavy, rusted chains. A similarly rusted lock that looked as if it could only be opened by a skeleton key tightly held the chains together. In the upper part of the door in the rounded section was a small glass-less window, no larger than maybe six inches square with one thin metal bar extending vertically in the center.

Nick glanced around to see if any other doors had magically appeared in the corridor. He couldn't locate any. As his head and eyes continued to scan the darkness Jeffrey continued, "Now, let's see. Whose room is this?" He placed a finger to his chin and thought, "I do believe this may be Sam." Jeffrey leaned in close to a small number plate recessed into the wood of the doorframe that looked as if it had been hand-chiseled from a piece of old granite, and he adjusted his glasses. "Ah, yes, room 19754438. It is Sam."

Jeffrey turned to Nick, whose attention he now had. "He likes to call himself 'Chubby' for some reason." Jeffrey looked back through the small window that was just at his eye level and continued to speak as he peered inside the room. "He's home." He looked down at Nick and chuckled, "Well, where else would he be?"

The window was too high for Nick, who attempted and failed to see through the tiny square, stretching his neck to its limit in the attempt.

"His crimes weren't like yours. I suppose, in comparison, they were more like mine." Jeffrey spoke as he continued to look through the tiny opening, "His pain is quite unique, though, as is everyone's. I think the Boss gets a kick out of him. You see, his punishment involves being dropped straight down a very tight, very long tube-like thing." Jeffrey looked down at Nick, "Like a children's plastic, tubular slide at a public park. Except that the sides are made up entirely of razor blades. He drops as the crow flies close to one full mile. Although it takes him a while to complete the fall, I must say. The blades catching on his flesh slow him down considerably, more than you'd think when you consider Newtonian mechanics." Jeffrey's smile widened, "There's really no need to make it a quick drop, now is there, when you consider that time isn't a factor? Anyway, when he reaches the bottom, or rather what's left of him, he lands in a cast iron hog scalder where he's eaten alive by a pack of wild jackals. And, I might add that he's still quite conscious throughout the ordeal.

Nick continued to test the limits of his height as he stood and his tiptoes, still not having the ability to see into the room.

"Well, when you think about it, he has to be alive and conscious during it, now doesn't he? He can't die again. And, he is required to be fully aware of the pain he's receiving through the duration of the event." Jeffrey peered back through the window, "You can't say the Boss doesn't have a sense of humor." Jeffrey's tone turned to one of concern, "I'm not certain I should let you see him, though. You may not be ready. It doesn't seem to be Sam's cycle anyway." He turned away from the window to look down at Nick again, "We should keep moving."

Nick's demeanor once again turned sour as he pointed at the door, shaking his finger. "I want to see in there! How do I know you aren't lying to me? How do I know that there isn't anyone in that room?! This is all just scare tactics to try to get me to believe something that isn't really there! Open that door!"

Jeffrey remained consistently calm and monotone, "Oh, my. There you go again with your anger. You really should learn to put that in check. It won't help you at all down here, Nicholas. And, to answer your question, you don't know that I'm not lying. You have no choice but to trust me as I told you before."

"Trust?! Are you kidding me?!"

"Look, I'm just trying to help you get accustomed to the place." Jeffrey attempted reasoning in his tone, even though it was received as belittling, "Think of it as an on-the-job training session. Don't you want to know how it all works before you earn your first paycheck? Wouldn't a bit of knowledge be helpful before you're left to your own thoughts? You don't want to simply be thrown to the wolves now do you?" Jeffrey paused, frowning behind his glasses before laughing out loud.

"What's so damn funny?!"

"Oh, nothing. That just made me think of Amelia. She's around here somewhere close by, I think." He shook his head, "It's disgusting what those wolves do to her, too. I'm glad that isn't my punishment. Oh, well, never mind."

Jeffrey's tone returned to one of reasoning, "Look, you've got nothing but eternity ahead of you. Why not spend these last few moments, pardon the reference again, walking along with me and trying to get something out of the conversation? It might just help you." Pointing down at Nick, "Not to mention, you're the one that pushed the down button, not me. You requested this floor, so why not try to learn a thing or two about where you are."

A surprised Nick's eyes opened wide behind his thick glasses, "What do you mean I chose this place?!"

"Well, you had three choices, didn't you?"

"I don't remember that!"

"You were staring straight at them when the elevator doors opened. Not to mention, you were the only one in the elevator, now, weren't you? Who else could have pushed that button?"

"I didn't think there were any buttons! Are you telling me I had a choice?!"

Jeffrey chuckled in his response, "Well, theoretically, you didn't. But, I suppose you could have tried. And, perhaps you even did. You're the one with the poor memory, not me. You very well could have stepped off on the top floor. But, let's face it, if you did you were shoved right back into the elevator. They can't be fooled, you know."

Nick's head snapped and his eyes went in the direction of where they'd walked from. He saw only a dimly lit, musky-smelling hallway with seemingly no end to it. "Where's the elevator?! We haven't walked that far! Where's the damn elevator?!" He turned back and looked up at Jeffrey and pointed, "I didn't push any buttons! I don't even remember getting into that death trap! Are you telling me I could have chosen to go up and not down?!"

"I suppose you could have. Like I said, maybe you even tried, for all I know. But, let's face it, there was no chance of getting off and remaining on *that* floor, now was there? Not with what you did. Your only destination was ultimately down here with us, regardless. Any choices that you could have made would still have brought you straight here."

A pathetic, sad look overtook Nick's face as he gazed down the tunnel again only to see walls, rafters, and flames flickering from the candles perched on the dozens of chandeliers that he could see, and the many more in the darkness that he could not. No elevator could be found.

"You still don't get it, do you? I told you before, there's no time down here. Just the place itself. You don't even realize how long you've been here since we've been walking together, now do you? Forgive the reference, if you will. I really must stop making mention of the concept of space and general relativity." Jeffrey began to ramble proudly, "You see, Nick, According to these theories, the concept of time depends on the spatial reference frame of the observer, and the human perception…"

"Just shut up! And, what do you mean? We've only been walking a couple of minutes." Nick's sarcasm had returned along with his anger as he squinted and continued to seek an elevator in the darkness, or anything for that matter.

"Oh, dear. There you go again not paying attention to what we're trying to tell you. Not to mention, your temperament. It's quite the bad habit, isn't it?" Jeffrey frowned and shook his head, "And, by habit, I'm making innuendo to your routine, regularly repeated behaviors. Not the thing that nuns wear. We don't talk about nuns or priests down here, for obvious reasons."

Nick looked back to his host and shook his head in disgust, "You're really pissing me off. Okay, fine, then tell me. How long have I been down here?"

Jeffrey's voice hinted disgust, "Well, then. Fine. I will tell you. But just you remember, time fundamentally doesn't exist here. It never did. Even when you were alive, time was relative, not absolute. But, I'll keep this simple so even you can understand."

"Just tell me how long!"

"It took you one hundred years to arrive at that first door where Sam's space was. Not to mention the additional year that you were riding on that elevator."

Nick's eyes widened and his mouth dropped open. He whispered, still with a biting tone, "You aren't serious, are you?"

"Who's to tell? I think I'm being serious." Jeffrey smirked, "You just need to trust me." He then looked at his wrist, which didn't have a watch on it. "We should keep going."

Nick didn't understand the metaphor, and neither did he care. He just kept staring in the direction he felt the elevator should have been and began instinctively to walk backward behind Jeffrey, nearly tripping over his own two feet.

"I still don't understand." The two kept a steady, slow pace in the uncomfortably warm corridor as they continued on their journey. The flames from the candelabras continually flickering off the dark walls provided a steady, but very low light, causing shadows to dance on the walls. Nick still believed that the cracks in the walls were glowing the same as the floor below from something behind it all. He doubted his eyes, though, and felt it may be that they were playing tricks on him.

Jeffrey stared straight ahead, "What's there to understand?"

"Who's down here? I mean, what's it take to get sent here? Are all the sinners here?"

"Of course not. Don't be silly, everyone's a sinner. We'd be bursting at the seams if that were the case. And believe me, there's still room down here for others, although not much. We're filling up fast these days. No, just the really terrible ones, like you. Those are the ones who end up here."

"What do you mean?"

"I told you, everyone sins. Don't you read? Everyone's born a sinner. Only the ones that do the things similar to you and I get stuck down here in this place. You know, the ones that made the conscious choices to harm others without cause. The ones that decided that the rules didn't apply to them. Things like that."

Nick appeared puzzled. "What do you mean harm without a cause? I considered myself to have a cause. So did you. Doesn't that count?"

"Certainly not. You killed others out of anger and stupidity. Although you mistakenly felt it was out of recognition. I killed out of lust, greed, ego, and power. We're the ones that end up here, not the others."

"Others? What others?"

Nick's teacher, with an arm remaining around the younger lad's shoulders, appeared annoyed that his student didn't seem to comprehend what was being told to him. "How can I explain this so that you'll understand?" He thought for a moment as they strolled, "Okay, let's try this. An army soldier shoots his enemy during wartime, right? He does this because that's what he was told to do by someone superior to him, even though his enemy is innocent of any crimes other than being an unwilling participant on the opposite side of the very same conflict. He's simply on the wrong team of the soldier that shoots him dead." Jeffrey looked down at Nick, "Does that mean the soldier who killed his enemy committed murder? Of course not. He did what he was told to do. He did what was instilled in him, right or wrong."

Jeffrey returned his focus forward, "That person doesn't end up here. He's absolved of any wrongdoing, and rightfully so. Even the person that ordered him to kill is absolved. The ones that bear the brunt are the person, or persons, ultimately in charge that started it all and didn't have the brains or the compassion to simply end it before it all began. The power-hungry ones who decided that for whatever reason, others needed to die for their cause. Although, it also depends on the reasons for taking the action to begin with, of course. And ultimately, how they make the decision to end the conflict."

Nick was unknowingly nodding his head as he stared at the floor beneath him, watching the cracks, striations, burns, and knotholes in the lumber's ancient design pass by underneath his feet. Still straining in an effort to determine what, if anything, was below. And for now, he listened.

"Or perhaps a police officer shoots and kills someone

that's threatening the life of an innocent person, or people. Or maybe someone shoots at the officer first, and that officer is required to return fire. That officer doesn't come here. In the end, the officer travels up in the elevator and all is forgiven. The obvious difference is those people didn't harm or take the lives of people for no reason whatsoever. Or, at least a reason that they were in control of. They were doing what society expected them or told them to do. In other words my dear Nick, they were doing their jobs."

"So, if I understand. Like the war thing, the one who started the war and stuff? They end up here?" For the first time on their journey, Nick's tone wasn't one of anger or sarcasm. For the moment he'd calmed and provided an indication that he was taking an interest.

"It depends. If it was retaliation for someone who acted first, then possibly not. However, if the conflict started out of anger, power, or greed? Then yes, of course, those decision makers will most likely end up here, if not purgatory first."

"Purgatory?"

"Yes, of course. Didn't you pay attention? What do you think that other choice was for in the elevator? Now, please Nick, let's try to stay on track, shall we?"

The two ceased walking and again Jeffrey turned to face the younger man, "Now, back to what we were talking about. If that army soldier goes out and kills randomly without an order to do so. Or, does it outside of the rules of war, like killing an innocent civilian and then attempting to use the conflict as an excuse for doing so? Yes, of course, they'll end up here. Just because you're placed, or volunteer, for a situation of struggle doesn't give you an excuse to act outside of the boundaries of normal, or expected behavior. You can't just decide to break the rules set forth by each, or any society."

"What if they only kill one person? Or just one sexual assault? Or their victim doesn't die? Will they still end up here?"

Jeffrey's expression turned to one of disgust. "That's a dumb question. Of course, they will. There's no minimum quota for criminal behavior. You can't commit an act of random violence just once and then expect that all will be forgiven if you promise to never do it again. It doesn't work that way, Nick. There are victims involved that expect, if not demand, a proper and just punishment in return for your actions. The Boss isn't going to keep count of how many you harm. Only that you willfully did it." Jeffrey raised a finger, "One life is more than enough, Nick."

Jeffrey prompted the two to begin strolling again, "Not to mention, the Boss simply wants you down here. And, there are plenty of good ones who travel up. Many more than we have down here, so no one's going to keep track of how many victims you create. Only that there are, in fact, victims. I mean, take a look at your crime, Nick. Do you really think if you'd gone into that school and only killed one child, or only one adult, that you wouldn't have ended up here? You were destined for permanent residency the moment you planned that terrible act, and carried out those plans. And, rightfully so." Jeffrey stuck his free arm out in gesture, "This place is the ultimate and just punishment. We need this place, Nick. Society needs this place. Let's face it, Societies have historically become so much worse at administering punishments to the wicked and guilty. Nobody gets what they really deserve from any modern culture's justice system, or even from their courts of public opinion. Although, between the two, the public generally does a better job at punishing in certain societies, now don't they? But, they haven't always gotten that right either."

"What do you mean?"

Jeffrey was relishing in the wisdom he was providing. He boasted, "Well, for example, take a look at the year 1692 and the Salem witch trials that took place during that period. They weren't really witches at all, now were they?" He pointed down at Nick, "But, they were still punished by the public and their judicial system, now weren't they? And, punished in the most brutal of ways for the time period in which they lived. So, of course, those who were accused of witchcraft didn't end up here just because they were found guilty by their magistrates. However, those that deemed them guilty and ordered their punishments? Oh yes, they ended up here. Especially those who knew the truth and still did nothing to stop it or make it right."

"Okay, fine, but many believed that witches did exist. And, those people believed they were doing what was right. Doesn't the time period make a difference? What about those people that thought they were doing what was right?"

Jeffrey looked down and gave Nick a dirty, frowning smirk. "Sort of sounds like you, now doesn't it? It doesn't have anything to do with the period in history. You believed in your cause and look where you ended up. Just because you believed that what you were doing was right didn't make it so. Nor was it an excuse, now was it? Well, then. There's your answer. And, it wasn't any more just for those fools that believed they were dealing with witches, now was it?"

Jeffrey looked to see if he could find any evidence of reasoning or understanding in Nick's expressions. He couldn't locate any as he continued, "Not to mention, don't you think it's even worse when it occurs over a period of time and the ones that are in power simply continue to make the same poor decisions when it comes to judgments and punishments? The witch trials, again, for instance. Don't you think that during that time period someone would have thought that what they were doing was wrong? That witches didn't really exist? But, no. In fact, it grew progressively worse. Every time someone didn't like their neighbor, or a business deal went bad, or even if they envied someone or became jealous, they accused the other person of being a witch. As a result, another innocent person was convicted. Those poor souls were thrown away into dungeons, or put to death. And for what reason? Out of pure superstition, or worse, for greed or envy. Nothing else."

Jeffery looked down and gestured again, "Think about it,

Nick. You could throw a living person away or even execute them in a public setting for no more than pointing a finger and calling that person a witch. All something that common sense tells us isn't true, without any real rhyme or reason. All because the time period led them to believe that witches existed. Think about it, Nick. People today still believe in witches, ghosts, and goblins, but that doesn't make it so. Talk about wasting the lives of innocent people. Not to mention that some of the condemned in Salem were children as young as five years old. Common sense should have told them that by the time they got to Martha Cory, they were doing something that was terribly wrong."

"I still say it was justified. They believed in what they were doing."

"Of course you do." Jeffrey's tone was pompous, "It's sad, really." Jeffrey halted the two, "Ah, speaking of witchcraft and other twisted beliefs, here we have the 15th century."

Jeffrey directed Nick to his left where, seemingly again out of nowhere, a new passageway had appeared. Nick's head snapped around, attempting to determine if any other passageways or doors had appeared, finding none. He then adjusted his glasses and peered down the new walkway. The corridor was identical to the one they had been traveling, with no end to be seen in the darkness beyond the flickering candlelight. Although, this time guttural moaning and screaming could be heard echoing throughout the endless vestibule, with some seemingly close by and quite loud, and others sounding in the distance, far away.

"Overzealous religious beliefs can be such a messy thing, don't you think?" Jeffrey mentioned as together the two men gazed down the newly discovered passageway. "Especially if you use it as some sort of weapon."

Jeffrey spoke as if he were responding to the sounds emitting from this particular tunnel, "Such a loud and obnoxious century. All the torturing and such." He glanced down at Nick. "Attempting to force one's religious beliefs on others never works out well in the end." They both looked back down the dimly lit black hole as Jeffrey continued, "No need to go down that way. It's quite overcrowded down there, and quite depressing. Let's move along."

"Wait! What's happening to them? Who are they?"

"They're the ones that tried to force their beliefs on others, of course. And, when I say force, I mean through means no less than torture and murder. However; not necessarily the ones that carried out the sentences. Again, you can't punish someone for doing their jobs, especially if they're going to receive similar punishment if they defy their master's orders to do so, as would possibly have been the case for those that carried out the executions and such. Torturers and executioners were, for the most part, just doing their jobs."

Jeffery peered back down the audible corridor. "No, no. Those down there are the ones who made the decisions to force change on others, or called for the punishments themselves." Jeffrey removed his glasses and began wiping them with a handkerchief that appeared from his shirt pocket as he continued to gaze in the direction of the screaming. "Historically they were known as tyrants. You know, heavy-handed rulers and their henchmen that forced their religious beliefs on others." He motioned to the hallway with the hand that held his glasses, "This particular century is sort of an exception to the rule too. These people really do receive the same forms of torture that they ordered to be inflicted on others. You know, they're being burned at the stake, stretched on the rack, strappados, the wheel, etcetera, etcetera. Those sort of things, over and over again." Jeffrey smiled down at Nick after returning his glasses to the bridge of his nose, "There was really no need for the Boss to come up with anything different than the pain they were dishing out to people that simply didn't think, or act, the way they wanted. They stood by and watched as innocent people received unbelievably long, painful forms of torture which almost always caused slow death that they themselves had ordered to be carried out. And, simply for reasons of power and greed. So, what's good for the goose is good for the gander, don't you think? Come along now, more to see and do." Jeffrey adjusted his glasses again and allowed the handkerchief to fall to the floor. Nick hadn't watched it drop to see that when it landed, it disappeared.

"Wait a minute!" Nick pointed down the audible corridor as they turned to walk away. "Okay, I kind of get it that these people deserve what they're getting. But, are you trying to tell me that religion doesn't also save people? I mean, what about people who find *Go*..." Nicholas corrected himself, closing his eyes in defeat, "I mean religion? You know, they do something bad and then turn to religion later on? What about those people? Isn't there supposed to be forgiveness for those people? I mean, maybe not to the ones down there that tried to force their belief on others. But, what about those people who turn to *Go*...." Nick shook his head, "I mean turn to religion?"

"Silly boy." Jeffrey was amused by the naïve nature of the question, "Do you really think that it's okay to torture or kill someone, and then claim that you've discovered..." Jeffrey pointed up and motioned with his eyes, "...in some pitiful attempt to get yourself out of trouble? That just because all of a sudden you declare that you've been saved through religious beliefs, that it was okay to have committed murder in the first place and leave victims behind to suffer? My dear boy, it doesn't work that way. You can't harm others and then blurt out that you've discovered the meaning of the big guy upstairs, and then expect to use that as an excuse to be pardoned for what you've done in the end."

Jeffrey's motions became animated again, "My goodness if that were the case everyone would go around committing horrendous, unimaginable crimes and then just blurt out that they've found...well, you know who." Jeffrey whispered the last line, motioning upwards with his eyes again before returning to his pompous tone, "That's such a cop-out if you ask me. It's just another excuse to try and get away with something. Or, to use as a last-ditch effort to avoid being sent down here when the end is nearing. No, no, that doesn't work. In fact, in my opinion, it only accelerates one's trip straight down on that foolish elevator that brought you and I here."

The two began their walk again at Jeffrey's prompting as he moved forward away from the newfound corridor, and Nick followed. "Think about it, excuses are a dime-a-dozen. Not to mention weak." Jeffrey puffed his chest, "Be a man instead, Nick! Take responsibility for what you've done. Don't you think a person who admits to their crimes is so much more honorable than the one who denies ever committing them? Own up to the atrocities that you've carried out, Nicholas, rather than trying to avoid them. Plead guilty and take your punishment. I mean, you did, now didn't you? You didn't claim that you were innocent. Your trial was only for the purpose of determining punishment. So, why on earth would you then pull a cowardly move like declaring that you discovered religion in some wretched effort to be saved? It doesn't make sense at all. Take your punishment like a man, for goodness sake!"

"I suppose." Nick looked up from the floor he'd been staring at again as he walked, "By the way, it was my defense team that suggested I plead guilty, not me."

"Of course it was. I understand."

Part 3
Nick Receives a Scolding

The two continued as Jeffrey attempted to keep Nick's attention focused, "Now, let's go over the next rule. And, I hate to disappoint you, but I feel the need to tell you that you won't be receiving answers to all of your questions. You gave up that privilege when you were sent here as part of your punishment. All those questions you may have had about the origins of humanity, or how the earth was created, or how it will all end? Or, who killed JFK? No, you won't receive any of the answers. In fact, the only questions you're allowed to ask along our little journey together must be restricted to this place alone. And, perhaps purgatory. And, I implore you, if you have questions, ask them now. Otherwise, once our little stroll is complete, no further inquiries will be satisfied. In fact, no further verbal contact with anyone, ever, will occur at that point."

Nick's attitude remained poor, "Good, I don't like talking to people anyway."

Jeffrey glanced down beside himself, an expression of disbelief overtaking his face.

The younger man looked up and noticed, "Okay, fine. Tell me, who's in purgatory?"

"Ah, well now, there are many types in that place. And, in general, the decor is quite the same as it is down here. You know, everyone in their own little space and all. The only difference is there are no actual punishments taking place. Well, other than the solitude itself, where they're left to deal with their own thoughts and ponder their life decisions and actions."

"Actions?"

"Yes, of course. They're not stuck there simply for no reason. They all did something. Something questionable that could ultimately either land them here or if they're lucky, they'll be allowed into the place that *he* dwells.

Nick was only half-heartedly interested, "Okay, so what kind of things get them sent to purgatory?"

"Well, let's see, there are many reasons. Ah, one, for example, your defense team. They're waiting there."

Nick stopped and looked up at his host with a bit of surprise, "My defense team? Why?"

Jeffrey ceased walking, turned, and addressed Nick, "Well, to be specific, just one of them. I mean, you can't necessarily punish people just because they're tasked with defending someone wretched like you. No, no, only that terrible lady who sat directly beside you during your sentencing trial, and joked with you." Jeffrey shook his head, "Quite wicked if you ask me. All those families in that courtroom watching the two of you smiling, laughing, and joking. It exemplified their pain and anguish terribly. And, not to mention, both of you were displaying the behavior on live television for everyone to see. Well, anyone who bothered to watch that puny, little streaming network, anyway." Jeffrey's eyebrows raised from behind his darkened spectacles, "The judge certainly wasn't pleased."

His host placed an arm back around the young man's shoulders and they began to walk again. "I mean, there you were, having committed all those murders. Children, for goodness sake. And there you two sat, smoking and joking while waiting to see what your sentence ultimately would be.

And, those poor, innocent families that were forced to sit in that courtroom and watch the two of you, both with smiles on your faces, giggling and laughing like it was all a joke. A terribly poor choice on her part, I must say. You, I expected no less. Yes, Nick, she's waiting there now, in purgatory. Pondering her ways, you might say."

"Waiting? What is she waiting for?"

"Yes, she's waiting. Waiting to see if she'll ultimately go up or down. Waiting with only her own thoughts to keep her company. And, ultimately, it will be her thoughts alone that will determine her outcome. Her fate will be decided by none other than herself. First, she must realize what it is that she's done and then decide whether she's apologetic or not. Or, if she even realizes why she's there, to begin with. She could simply be sitting there in denial for a very, very long time."

"How long will it take for her to figure it out?"

"Oh, dear, that *time* thing again. Well, I suppose that was my fault by making mention of it. To be honest, I don't know. She's still there now, sitting, suffering in her own solitude, and thinking."

Nick stopped to look up and face Jeffrey, "Wait a minute! She's there now?! She was alive when I was executed. How can she be in purgatory now? That would mean that she's dead!"

Jeffrey closed his eyes and shook his head. "Come, now, Nick. Really? Have you completely forgotten our little talk about how long you've been here thus far? She's been dead many, many years now. Well, I say years only again as a reference to the atomic clock, or the system of coordinated universal time, if that suits you better. Time in purgatory means no more than it does here, except for maybe the fact that there will be a moment during her eternity when she either goes up or down for the duration of her stay. Other than that one single moment in which she makes the right or wrong choice, time means no more to her than it does to you here now.

Agitation returned along with a bit of defeat and Nick rubbed his eyes under his glasses, "Okay, fine. Whatever. So, they just sit there and think? Am I understanding this correctly? If they feel sorry about what they did, they are forgiven?"

"If they understand what it was that they did, and they are truly sorry? Then most certainly, yes. It's like a game of chance. The Boss and the big guy betting against each other to see who gets to keep the soul of the person in wait. I will say, that not many win at that game. I mean, if we're looking at it in the sense of winners versus losers, they usually roll craps. And, the Boss so enjoys it when the big guy loses one."

"So, she just sits there. No hints about what she did as a reminder?"

"Well now, that would be cheating, wouldn't it? No, no. They're left to their own pathetically weak memories of what they did during their lives. And, I say weak in that if they'd been smart and strong in the first place, they wouldn't have committed their mistakes to be ultimately sent there." Jeffrey continued, "Your defense attorney, for example. If she'd had one, tiny bit of logic in her feeble little brain, she never would have joked with you in the courtroom with all those families present to see it happen. My goodness, those poor people had to sit there in that courtroom for weeks on end along with the person who'd mowed down their children with an automatic rifle like they were blades of grass under a lawnmower. And then to see that same evil tyrant smiling and joking with his own defense attorney?" Jeffrey's voice had raised in his excited state and he was forced to calm himself, "She deserves to be there, Nick. They all do. And, whether or not they're truly sorry for what they've done and not just the fact that they realize what their actions were. That's a big part of it. I'm telling you, Nick, if she doesn't figure it out soon, she'll find herself right down here with all the others."

"I don't think that's right. She didn't do anything

wrong."

"Well now, it's not up to you."

Nick's tone was one of disappointment, "Fine. So, who else is there?"

"Well, let's see. Oh!" Jeffrey perked up and pointed at Nick, "There's a large population of chronic substance abusers waiting there. They make up a good portion of the population."

Nick's surprise was apparent, "What? People who do drugs? How can that be?!"

"Oh, please, you aren't going to go into a speech about it being society's fault, now are you? And, I said chronic abusers. Those feeble-minded souls that were given every chance to quit their disgusting habits. And, let's face it, it was a choice, now wasn't it?"

"But, I thought…"

Jeffrey cut Nick's words short, "Your first mistake. Come, now. Drugs were a choice. And, shame on your generation that blamed everyone other than the users." Jeffrey's tone turned to whining, "It was their parents. It was their friends. It was the doctors." He regained his composure, "That last one makes me laugh the heartiest. The medical profession got blamed only because society failed at every other excuse and refused to lay blame on the source. It's quite amusing, really. Your society couldn't fix the problem, and they'd already used a laundry list of excuses for generations before them, so they simply created another reason for the problem. No, rather than blame the source, which was the user themselves, they laid the blame on modern medical practices. Shame on them."

Jeffrey's whining tone remained, "I mean, really. Someone sought out medical attention for an issue and then blamed their physician when they got hooked? Come, now, wasn't that what the doctor was supposed to do? Weren't they supposed to administer and prescribe narcotics for pain, a stimulant for anxiety, or anti-depressants for chronic depression?" Jeffrey's animated hands flew into the air,

"What were the doctors supposed to do when every Tom, Dick, and Harry came into their office complaining that their pinky hurt? Wave a magic wand and tell them they were all better?" He pointed down at Nick, "Did the medical providers advise their patients to crush it up and snort it up their noses, or melt it all down and inject it into their veins? No, they didn't! And, treating the substance abuse like it was something new that hadn't already been around for generations? Just shameful."

The host lowered his arms back down in defeat. "By the time your generation came around drug use had been a part of society for hundreds, if not thousands of years. To suddenly label it as an epidemic or a medical problem was truly weak." Jeffrey peered down and perked back up, "I'm curious, what are your thoughts on this subject, Nick?"

"I don't know."

Jeffrey's head snapped back up and he raised a finger, "Of course, you don't. Well, then, I'll tell you. Your generation turned all the chronic abusers into the 'boys that all cried wolf'. They allowed everyone else to be blamed rather than the individual themselves. Now, I ask you, what did that teach anyone? And the result?" Jeffrey pointed down at the young man again, "The result was, as I'd mentioned, that the medical profession began calling it an illness. Or, even worse, a disease. Like drug addiction was some sort of cancer, a head cold, or an auto-immune disorder that might be cured by modern medicines. Even worse, they attempted to label every user as someone with a mental illness that the drugs caused. Terrible, if you ask me."

The two began to stroll again. "So, the chronic users destroyed not only their own lives, but those of their families and friends, and even people they didn't know. They committed crimes against society to support their weaknesses, or worse, even stole from their loved ones. And, denied all of it. All the while claiming that they didn't even have a problem, to begin with, or lied and told everyone they had it under control. They made excuses for themselves while continuing to hurt and destroy others. Are you understanding this at all, Nicholas?" Jeffrey glanced down for his answer.

"No." Nick's head never looked up from the floor that he continued to watch it go by underneath his feet.

Jeffrey's head snapped back up as they strolled. "Ah, well, I thought not. Allow me to attempt to explain further. Let's see," Jeffrey thought and then gestured into the air. "Ah, yes, here we go. You have two people, similar in age, gender, and all the other particulars that make up the human form. Neither person having a history of any illnesses, mental, physical, or otherwise. However, both require medical attention for something." Jeffrey pointed to his pupil, "Let's say they both shatter their knees playing football. Now, the doctor prescribes the same type of medications to both, equal prescriptions as far as the type of narcotic, dosages, and length of practical use."

Jeffrey looked down at Nick as they continued to walk, "In time both men heal from their afflictions, but let's go as far as to say both with some sort of chronic pain in the aftermath. Even just only mild pain, let's say. Now, one becomes addicted to the drug that the doctor prescribed, and the other doesn't. The second person chooses alternatives. Perhaps exercise or physical therapy. Or maybe some other form of pleasure or pastime to keep their mind off the pain, or to manage it over time. A hobby or something. Or, perhaps they simply choose to deal with the pain. Now, are you going to blame society for the first one that chose to destroy his life, and the lives of others by remaining addicted to a chemical? Is it society's fault that he made the wrong choice while the other made the correct one?"

Jeffrey hesitated for a moment, waiting on an answer from Nick, which did not come. "So, then. One remains strong-minded and the other chooses the weak approach. And, by his chosen action, he causes a life of pain to not only himself but also pain and anguish to those around him." Jeffrey perked up, "Well now, Nicholas, if that be the case, in the end, the weak ones are placed in purgatory to sit and think." Jeffrey glanced down again as they strolled, "And, again Nick. If they make the correct decision, they're allowed to push that 'up' button that you so now covet. Not to mention, those who are still alive and, ultimately make the correct choice to not abuse, or stop taking the chemicals altogether? Yes, they are forgiven before their end comes." His host spoke sternly, "In other words, Nick, we ultimately get all of the weak-minded ones down here, and the strong-willed are allowed to move to the kingdom located on the upper floor. Do you now understand?"

"I suppose. Actually, I don't really care."

Jeffrey ignored the remark as he continued arrogantly, "Ah, now, the drug dealers! Yes, of course, they all come here. There's no passing go, no collecting their two-hundred dollars. Just straight here. They're the ones that have chosen to harm others for profit. It's simple, Nick. It doesn't matter whether you're the guy who sells to kids in a schoolyard or the leader of a large cartel. There's no gray area, and certainly no rehabilitation for those types. Selling a chemical that alters the mind, destroys the body, and kills earns you a one-way ticket here." Jeffrey chuckled, "Rehabilitation. Another gray area, if you ask me. Your society, for example, attempting to force rehabilitation on those weak-minded fools that used or sold drugs as a substitute for a real punishment. Society itself was the only one being punished by that thought process. True rehabilitation only comes from one place, the individual. There is no forcing it. Don't you agree?"

"I don't know. Who cares?" Nick's tone was certainly proving to Jeffrey that the young lad, in fact, didn't care as he continued, "Who else is there? In purgatory, I mean."

"Well, let's see. Oh, yes, here's one that will interest you. The fanatic gun advocates. Primarily from your generation. Many of them are waiting there."

"Gun nuts? Why?"

"Just the real extremists. Even worse if they were politicians too. You know, the decision-makers. The ones that would argue regardless of how many innocent children died by the likes of people like you. Those that would twist the Second Amendment into something it wasn't intended to be to suit their own purposes, even if their own family members were shot and killed. Yes, they're in purgatory."

"I don't get it. Why?"

"Oh, come now, Nick. This one shouldn't surprise you. And, remember, I said the staunch fanatics." Jeffrey's tone turned to reason, "Think about it, Nick. Those fools that touted the right to bear any type of arms even when people around them were dying at the hands of those who chose to randomly kill children with guns they shouldn't have possessed in the first place. Those that refused to even hold a conversation, or worse, turned their backs when victims were begging for society's laws to be changed, or even simply a compromise. Those fools that stood and looked the parents of dead children straight in the eye and made excuses, causing those mothers and fathers even more pain. Of course, they're sitting and contemplating their actions. I mean, really, not even willing to hold an adult conversation on the matter? Or worse, promising those same parents to their faces that they would do something only to mock them and do absolutely nothing, and then defend that very action."

"Guns are a right."

"Silly boy. Guns were no more a right than driving a car ever was. They were a privilege, at best. A privilege meant to be earned. But, of course, you'd think that way. Look at what you used to commit your crime. Now, I ask you, were you a big game hunter? Did you target practice regularly in any gun club? Were you seeking to protect yourself, or your family with that assault rifle? Did you live in a high-crime area? Did you take a firearm safety course? Did you have a job that required you to own a gun? Were you a veteran?"

Jeffrey turned to Nick and poked him in the shoulder, "The answer is 'no' to all of those. You purchased that weapon for the sole purpose of killing others. And, for those decision-makers that would defend your right to possess that gun even after the crime you committed through the use of it? Yes, they're contemplating those decisions right now in the middle plain. And, my guess is, they won't win that poker hand."

"Yeah, okay. But, they would argue that it was me that killed those kids and not the gun."

Jeffrey shook his head, "Exactly. And, how silly and outrageous is that excuse? What do you think, Nick? Did you kill them or the gun? I'd say it was the combination of the two. Without one working hand-in-hand with the other, those children would still be alive and you might not be here talking to me. Now, isn't that correct?"

"I could have chosen to use a knife."

Nick's poor attempt at reasoning had little effect on his host. "But, you didn't, now did you? You chose the weapon. And why a gun over a knife? Isn't it quite obvious, Nick? Body count, that's why. And, it was oh, so easy to obtain that gun, now wasn't it? Even the likes of you had no problem."

"Whatever. I think you're lying to me about all this."

"Maybe I am, Nick."

◆ ◆ ◆

Jeffrey stopped and turned to face Nick again. His tone turned to one of not entirely anger, but more of a demeaning, annoyed tone, "And, that's another thing. What is it with you school shooters? You completely embarrass us all. You're all so pathetic in your actions. You put no thought whatsoever into your crimes. You go out, buy a gun, maybe fill a duffle bag with ammunition and then walk into a school and shoot up the place. You don't even target just the ones that made you feel small, do you? You go after everyone. And, your entire crime is over almost before it begins." Jeffrey put a hand to his own chest, "For goodness sake, Nick, my achievements took years to plan out and execute." He pointed, "People like you? Your all done in just a few, short minutes."

Nick simply glared up at Jeffrey, taking in his comments with no visible expression behind his thick glasses.

"I mean, really. Most of you simply end up with your own gun in your mouth before it's all over. It's all so cowardly." A sarcastically pompous Jeffrey motioned to the young man, "Just look at yourself. You would've done the same thing if the cops hadn't gotten to you first. In essence, you failed at even that! And, for what? What did you ultimately get out of it? Please tell me, Nick. I'd really like to know."

Nick didn't offer a response, he simply stared blankly back up at the man who was scolding him.

"I'll tell you what." Poking the younger man in his chest, "Nothing, that's what. You all think that you're going to gain notoriety and be famous. Like some movie star or something. That was truly your only goal. Well, let me tell you something just in case you hadn't figured it out yet. It doesn't happen! It never happens! I'd be willing to bet right now that you can't even name another school shooter off the top of your head, can you? Well, guess what, Sunshine? If you can't, it's for certain nobody else in your world can either. And, not one of you has figured out that little tidbit of information. You all just keep trying and trying. And, ultimately, you all fail at it. Quite miserably, I might add."

Nick raised an eyebrow, appearing only to be a bit annoyed with the words coming from his host.

Jeffrey's demeaning tone continued. "For example, take a look at *your* achievement. Once your sentencing was over and that cell door slammed shut behind you for the final time, you fell into total obscurity with all the others just like you, whether dead or alive. In fact, the spotlight was off you only days after your little incident when the next one came along and did the same exact thing somewhere else. You didn't even get fifteen minutes of fame, to quote Warhol. You truly gained no notoriety in the form of stardom whatsoever. You're all truly pathetic and weak! In fact, the only notoriety that you yourself ever received were those ridiculous letters sent to you in prison from people just as sad, pathetic, and miserable as you. Is that what you strived for? Love letters from those even more feeble-minded than you were, all sent from their parent's basements?!"

Nick just continued his blank stare with his head cocked to one side. Although, his frustration was growing.

Jeffrey chuckled arrogantly, "And, don't you think it's ironic? Not only are none of you famous at all, but after your types are all lying dead on the floor from shooting yourselves in the heads, other people who were there become more well-known than any of you. I mean, with people like you dead and gone, the families and society begin to blame everyone else. The cops, the school officials, the lawmakers. The spotlight's on them, not you! And, all because the tiny, little no-names like you aren't alive anymore to blame."

Jeffrey's arrogant smile was wide, "So, everyone else gains unwanted notoriety by falling victim for what society claims were their inability to protect the children rather than the blame being placed on the shooters themselves. It's actually quite amusing, Nick! Your type falls into more obscurity by committing your crime than any notoriety you were seeking to gain in the first place! How hilarious is that?!"

Jeffrey's head flew backward and he uttered a cackling laugh before looking back to his pupil. "You're all so weak and deplorable! And, the fact that none of you ever figure any of this out in advance makes you all such sorry excuses for human beings!"

"Are you finished?" The calmly spoken question came with more than a hint of sarcasm from Nick.

Regaining composure and in a calmer tone, but still quite

pompous, "No, I'm not. You just don't get it, do you? Your kind doesn't even have a genre like we do. You simply fall into the same category as those racist idiots that drive their vehicles into parades, or those fools that go out and kill their fellow employees after being fired from a job that they couldn't handle in the first place. I mean, really. You didn't become famous at all. And, just think about it, Nick. By the time you committed your crime, there were hundreds of other incidents that occurred before yours in that same decade alone, and many more to come after yours. Plus the thousands over time before and after you. Not to mention, nobody knows who any of you are! Just the results of your carnage, but certainly not your name!

Nick faked a yawn.

Jeffrey's tone remained one of proud arrogance, "Look at me, for example. They made movies about me, dozens of documentaries, interviews, books have been written." The host checked his fingernails as if that were a symbol of status, "I've been a character in countless television horror series. For goodness sake, just look at what they did with my brain after my death. I'm a household name, Nick." He looked beyond his hand down to the younger man, "But you, Nicholas? Nothing. Nothing at all. Just another number in the criminal justice system until they laid you on that gurney and pumped you full of potassium chloride." Jeffrey shook his head slowly before turning to continue their walk. "Your kind truly disgusts me."

Nick cocked his head again and scratched his left eyebrow under his glasses, entirely unimpressed and seemingly unphased by Jeffrey's observations. He contemplated ending their walk to nowhere right then and there, having heard enough of the belittling he was receiving. He turned and peered down the dark hallway, thinking twice about bolting given the fact that where he believed he'd come from looked no different than where he believed they were headed. In fact, at that point, Nick didn't exactly know which direction they had, in fact, come from, or which way they were going. He stared in the direction he believed the elevator might be, seeing nothing but emptiness within a black hole that was the corridor.

"Are you coming, or what? We have more to see and talk about." Nick looked back to see Jeffrey just ahead of him had turned to ask the question. One more look around and Nick reluctantly followed as Jeffrey again extended an arm around the younger man's shoulders and guided him in the only direction he was destined to go.

Part 4

The Details

*N*ick's anger and frustration continued to churn in his gut as the two continued on their journey together.

"Alright, fine! So, tell me, who else is down here?"

Jeffrey looked down with another disappointed look on his face in response to the inquiry. Or more so, the tone in which it was asked. "What on earth do you mean? Don't tell me that you haven't figured *that* out yet?" Jeffrey stared straight in the direction they were continuing and changed his own tone to one of amusement, "I tell you what. Let's try this. You guess who's down here. You name someone that you might suspect has permanent residency and I'll let you know if they're here or not. That's fair, now isn't it? We'll make a game of it."

Nick's annoyance as they continued was obvious, and he remarked quite sarcastically, "Fine. Adolph Hitler."

Jeffrey chuckled, "Oh, come now. That's too easy. He's in room 19341945. In fact, the entire Nazi party practically has their own wing."

"Okay, what about Vladimir Putin."

"The room next to Hitler's. Of course, he isn't aware of

that fact, just the same as you won't know who's in the space next to you. Come on, now, Nicholas. Pick your brain. Try a harder one."

"Manuel Noriega."

Jeffrey placed a finger to his chin and looked up, "*Hmmm*, yes. Not far from here actually. He's in the south wing, I think."

"Pope John Paul."

"Are you trying to be funny?"

"Okay, fine. Ted Bundy."

"You're far too simple-minded. Didn't you pay attention in history class? Can't you come up with someone more interesting? For goodness sake, make this more challenging. Of course, Ted is in my section, as are all the serial murderers."

"Okay, then, how about Aileen Wuornos?"

Jeffrey rolled his eyes. "You don't listen very well, do you? Okay, then. Yes, of course. Now, I must say, she's an interesting case. I mean, if there were an argument at all as far as society being to blame, I suppose she'd have a defense. You know, poor childhood and all. Abandoned by her family. Living on the streets and prostituting herself. She began at an early age and later used it as a way to make money to support her lover, and then as a way to choose her victims. You know, the whole 'men are to blame' thing. Still, all of her choices could have been different. And, the Boss simply despises excuses. Plus, the whole *crazy* defense."

Jeffrey spoke as if providing a lecture to a classroom on the topic of the human mind, "I mean, technically she was insane, not just acting. But, that came later towards the end. In all actuality, she knew exactly what she was doing, as we all did. Not to mention that she didn't deny any of it. She took full responsibility for the murders, only blaming the men, and ultimately society. But even then, she wasn't very believable. It was the sociopathy that convinced her that she was defending herself when in fact she was lashing out against men in general."

"Thanks for the history lesson," Nick's tone was saucy. "So, what's her punishment?" The question was uttered with Nick still only partially listening, as he was dragging his fingernails on the dank walls. Most of Jeffrey's words were traveling straight through as he watched his own hand glide along. He pulled his hand back quickly when the first splinter slid under a fingernail, causing a sharp pain.

"Ah, now that's an interesting one." Jeffrey's smile widened, "And, you have to thank ancient Greece for her form of pain and punishment. Not to mention, Perilaus himself, even if you don't. Now, to elaborate, Aileen receives a form of the brazen bull. Although, not really a bull, but rather in the form of a human man. Ironic, don't you think? If you're not familiar, allow me to explain."

Jeffrey's eyes widened and his amused smile turned a bit evil. He spoke as if he were proud to be part of the conversation, and possibly a creator of the torture device itself. He became animated with his hands again, removing his arm from Nick's shoulder, "You see, Nick, she is made to crawl into a tight-fitting, hollowed-out bronze statue of a man. Through the ass-end, of course. Once inside, in her contorted discomfort, the pyres are lit underneath her. She cooks slowly, fully conscious and aware, with nowhere to go. There's no escape. She sizzles and fries and screams quite terribly throughout the ordeal while her skin bubbles and boils. Once she's well done, so to speak," Jeffrey chuckled, "she's removed from the device. She's then laid out on the ground, her eyes and nerves well intact and working as they should. Smoke rises from her incinerated body while she continues to cry out terribly, although she no longer has the ability to move with her limbs and joints all contorted in her state of crispness."

"What happens next?" Nick's enthusiasm was eerie as he was attempting to suck the splinter out of his finger.

"Ah, well that's when the hordes of swine arrive and have a good meal. Beginning at her feet, they work their way up while she watches, and feels her burnt flesh, tendons, muscles, and internal organs being ripped and torn away by their razor-sharp teeth."

Jeffrey leaned to his student, "A bit of irony there, I'm afraid. I'm told she was quite fond of bacon when she was alive." He stood back straight, "Anyway, after they make their way to her head and there's nothing else left other than a bit of bone and nerves below her neck she finds herself returned to her space, with only her thoughts of when it will occur again."

Nick giggled to himself and unconsciously shook his head. Although not entirely understanding the methodology of the torture device, he understood the results and seemed to enjoy the visual. This didn't go unnoticed by his host, who frowned before looking around and continuing, "Speaking of Perilaus and Phalaris, I believe they're around here somewhere."

"Who?"

"Never mind. So, as you can see, the mental illness defense doesn't work down here. As blaming society doesn't work, either. It's just another cowardly attempt to justify one's actions. And, it's not up to the individual, now is it? Nor the judge, magistrate, or jury. It's all up to the Boss in the end as to what the appropriate punishments shall be."

After taking another step or two Jeffrey stopped. To his right another door had appeared out of nowhere. "Now, take Ed here for example."

Once again, Nick's bewildered expression overtook him as he glared at the newfound door, the same design as the first with the top rounded and small window above Nick's eye level. He failed in another attempt to see inside the tiny opening as he stretched his body out.

Jeffrey easily peered through the window as he spoke into it, "Ed is undeniably insane, and most certainly a product of his parents. I mean, the constant belittling and neglect. Not to mention being made to wear girls' clothing as a child. Plus, the physical abuse. However, it's still not an excuse. How one chooses to grow up and escape all that is up to the individual. Nor can you blame his sexual preferences, either. He did what he did, fully aware of what he was doing, and that his actions were wrong."

Jeffrey pulled Nick along with his arm around his shoulders again as the young man strained to look back at the door he was being drawn away from.

"Wait, who is he? What did he do?"

Jeffrey paused, turning his head to look back, and spoke quite nonchalantly, "Who? Ed? Oh, not much. He just kept his mother's dead body in a room after digging her corpse out of the grave she'd been buried in. That, and the fact that he killed several women, skinned them, and made lampshades and other household items out of their flesh and bones. Nothing, really. Come along, now."

As the two walked away, Nick still strained to look back at the doorway. "So what does he get?"

Calmly, in monotone and with his signature smirk, "Well, let's just say to begin with he's forced to consume things that would even make me sick. I mean really nasty stuff. And, when I say forced, I mean there are metal restraints, plus the intubation to make certain he swallows everything without missing a bite, other than what he coughs up around the tubing. Oh, and don't think for a moment that the tube blocks his taste buds. He smells and tastes every bit of it." Jeffrey placed a finger to his chin and squinted, "I also believe his fingers and toes are being removed by the use of some type of garden shears while it's occurring, too. Plus, a castration by use of a spike and hammer to top it all off. Of course, the gagging and coughing make it difficult for him to scream out in pain. He gives it a valiant effort, though."

As Nick turned his head forward again and the door behind him disappeared without his knowledge. For the second time since arriving, Nick experienced a slightly queasy feeling in the pit of his stomach to his host's description.

♦ ♦ ♦

"I mean, speaking of serial murders, for example. A topic that I'm quite fond of, by the way, it doesn't matter what the demographic profile is. Whether it be out of anger, greed, lust, power and control, thrill, or attention seeking, it's still all the same. Well, except maybe those necrophiliac sickos or the cannibals." Jeffrey chortled, "Present company excepted, of course. However, there are still no excuses, we're all aware of what we're doing, whether we're insane or not."

The two continued their walk down the dimly lit, musty, and terribly uncomfortable passageway. Both, for the moment, spoke casually as if they were discussing the weather.

"Okay, but what about people like Charles Manson? What about his followers? Weren't they just doing what they were told?"

"Oh, come now, we've discussed this already. Being weak-minded isn't an excuse. And, what is mind-control, or brainwashing if you prefer, at its core? Is it real for everyone, or is it a product of being feeble-minded? Now, I ask you, are you really attempting to tell me that people like Tex Watkins, Susan Atkins, Linda Kasabian, or even that pathetic Patricia Krenwinkel didn't have the ability to make better choices? Was Manson holding their hands when they sliced that poor woman open and removed her unborn child from her abdomen? Was it Manson who wrote the messages on the walls in their victim's blood? Couldn't they all have just walked away without committing any of the murders? Of course, they could have. Manson wasn't with them at the Polanski house. They could have driven past and never looked back. But, they didn't."

"So, Manson is down here, right?"

"Obviously. That's a stupid question, Nick. Terribly stupid, if you ask me."

"Screw you! What's his punishment?"

"You seem to be awfully interested in what types of pain others are enduring down here, aren't you? It would seem to me that you should be worried about yourself, and not the others, Nick."

Nick's annoyance was apparent in his tone, "Just tell me."

Jeffrey smiled, "Oh, definitely one for the books. And, I so adore the Iron Maiden, now, don't you?" He spoke belittlingly, "You do know what that is, don't you Nick?"

"I…"

Jeffrey cut him off, "I thought not. It's such an interesting device. And, his is based on the Nuremberg model, of course. Plus, with the executioner always being a black man adds just a hint of finesse, don't you agree? And, obviously, Charles isn't allowed to make a sound or yell out his usual obscenities as the spikes penetrate his body."

Jeffrey was eerily eager to explain, "You see, first his tongue is ripped out slowly by the executioner, who uses a very dull blade. Of course, after it's all over he gets it back, only to have it torn out again during the next cycle. That was important to the Boss, for him to not have the ability to cry out or utter anything at all during the process, which as you know was something Charles so enjoyed doing during his existence. Speaking of that," as Jeffrey pointed and abruptly changed the subject, "we should discuss cult leaders before our walk is over. They're an interesting topic."

"Is that it? Just losing his tongue and some spikes?!"

Jeffrey stopped and looked down at Nick with amused bewilderment on his face. "Is that it? *Is that it?!* I'm sorry, are we boring you?" Jeffrey cocked an eyebrow and bent down to Nick's level, "Have you ever experienced the slow, fully conscious sensation of the Iron Maiden after having your tongue painfully removed? Have you felt iron spikes slowly penetrate your every internal organ, over and over again for all eternity while not having the ability to cry out through the mouthful of torn flesh and blood trickling down your chin?

Jeffrey stood straight. "Well, to begin with, I hadn't finished speaking before you felt the need to interject, now had I? And, no. That's not all. In fact, there's quite a bit more. Not that I'm going to tell you now, but really? Interrupting is so terribly rude, Nicholas. Are you growing weary of our walk? Is it not stimulating your senses enough? Are you not learning something, Nick?"

"I just thought his punishment should be more."

"Oh, now you're in charge, are you? You're making the decisions now?" Jeffrey's snarky tone returned to one of arrogant sensibility, "And I sincerely hope you're not under the impression that punishments are based on the overall scale of the horror that the individual has committed against others. I mean, you don't believe that someone like Charles Manson gets off easier than someone like Caligula, for example? Remember, Nick, everyone starts with a baseline punishment and they themselves determine if it will get worse."

Jeffrey poked Nick in his forehead, which annoyed the young man immensely, "And, don't think for one moment in that tiny little brain of yours that your pain is going to start out any different than what began for tyrants the likes of Little Boots or King Jie, or even Harmodius for that matter. Your pain will be immense, as theirs is, and will only grow worse based on your own ability to play, or rather not play by the rules down here."

Nick pushed Jeffrey's hand away before being poked again. "I thought you said…"

"Well," interrupting the younger man, "there you go, thinking again. Another bad habit of yours."

His host laughed it off, placed his arm back around Nick's shoulders, and led him on. The younger lad shook his shoulders but still allowed himself to be guided along as he made the observation, "Why's it so damn hot down here, anyway?"

Jeffrey stopped again, frowned while looking forward, and then let out a hearty laugh. "That's a good one, Nicholas! I am truly amused by that! May I use that sometime?"

Nick shook his head again, not fully understanding the satire associated with his inquiry. "Sure, go ahead."

◆ ◆ ◆

"So, what's Hitler's punishment, anyway?" Nick was staring up at the flickering lights emitting from the candelabras while being guided along by his host.

"Ah, now there's an interesting case." Jeffrey smiled, looking straight ahead as they walked together, "Now, let's see if I can recall. When his cycle arrives, I believe he finds himself on the guillotine, forced to kneel with his hands bound behind his back. His body is turned around, made to look up and watch the heavy blade fall from many feet high above. And, it falls almost as if in slow motion. Once the blade slices his neck, his severed head bounces down to the hot pavement below. As it wobbles to a stop, face up, he continues to watch as exactly one-thousand men, one by one, approach. Each one stands above his body-less head and he receives the Swedish Drink, or *Schwedentrunk*, if you will."

"What's that?"

"Ah, well, each man urinates and defecates on his head as he gags and chokes. He's quite unable to scream with his vocal cords having been severed by the blade." Jeffrey chuckled, "Not to mention what's trickling down what's left of his throat and oozing out onto the ground." Jeffrey was animated as he boasted, "Of course, as his eyes dart from side to side he sees that his surroundings resemble one of his own concentration camps. And, when he looks up, and when the piss and shit isn't drowning his eyes, he sees that every man bears the tattoo of someone he himself had ordered imprisoned. Just an added bonus to enhance the humiliation."

Jeffrey whispered and stated amusingly, "There's other things still happening to his headless body that he, no less, remains aware of and endures also." Jeffrey's voice returned, "Finally, after the last man has completed their task on his head, a giddy woman very much resembling Eva Brawn kicks it all over a battlefield, similar to kicking a soccer ball. Each time his head bounces, the nerve endings dangling from his neck send exquisitely sensitive messages to his brain and the pain is simply astounding. Finally, an SS tank drives over and crushes his head. It's all very disgusting and marvelous. And, quite amusing."

"Sweet!" Nick's enthusiasm visibly annoyed Jeffrey, who was genuinely concerned that his pupil was again missing the point. "Can I watch that?"

"No, you can't." The answer was direct.

Nick's enthusiasm reverted to frustration, "Why not?!"

"Because, my dear Nicholas, you want it too much. Which, by the way, brings me to our next little rule. You aren't allowed any pleasure or satisfaction down here. None. In fact, the lack of pleasure will cause you great distress and pain itself."

Nick was genuinely annoyed, "What do you mean?"

Jeffrey stopped again, appearing agitated at the inquiry, and he turned to face Nick. He sighed and spoke sternly, "Think about where you are. Do you really believe that you're to be allowed any form of satisfaction here? You just don't get it, do you? I'm talking about stimulation! You simply aren't allowed any. None at all." Jeffrey placed a finger to the young man's chest, "Oh, you'll be teased and feel the urges to the point of great mental anguish, but you'll receive no satisfaction to ease the sensations at all. Not ever." Jeffrey lowered his hand and flicked a finger to Nick's crotch.

Nick glanced down at himself with his eyes growing from behind his glasses, "Are you talking about sex?"

"Duh." Jeffrey's arrogance returned in his tone, "What

did you think I was talking about? Eating a delicious meal?" Jeffrey's eyes rolled and he smiled, "Well, there is that too. But yes, no sex, of any kind. It doesn't matter what your preference was, male or female."

Jeffrey's tone returned to a calming voice, "Oh, as I said, you will have the urges. And, not in the form you may think you will. There are no movies playing to arouse you. No magazines to look at. No, no, it's all just a feeling that the Boss will force upon you at whim. The urges will wash down over you like a waterfall, and they'll grow worse as you sit there to the point that you'll wish to go mad. However, with no more sexual organs to act upon the feelings, you'll simply suffer, greatly, in your urges that you can never satisfy."

Nick's eyelashes touched his brow as he looked back up at Jeffrey, "Do you mean to tell me...?" Nick's hand slowly slid to his lower abdomen where his genitals were once located.

Jeffrey smiled wide and his amusement was apparent, "That's right, Sunshine, nothing down there to jerk off anymore. All gone. You're a Ken doll now. Or a Barbie, if that's how you chose to identify."

Nick's other hand dropped to his midsection as he frantically searched through his corduroys in an attempt to locate that appendage that was once there. His head dropped down again. "What the fuck?! Where is it?!" Snapping his head back up, "This is some kind of bullshit!"

Jeffrey laughed, "I told you, there's no pleasure to be experienced down here. That luxury, along with many others, is now gone. Absolutely no feelings of satisfaction to be had. In other words, Nick, nothing to play with."

Jeffrey resumed walking as Nick frantically searched through his trousers for his genitalia.

His host called back, "You also won't eat or drink anymore. Oh, you'll have all of the pains, hunger, thirst, lust, the sensation of having to empty your bowels, an itch you can never scratch. You know, any sensation that you can imagine. And, each time you think about one," Jeffrey turned his head, "and you have all of eternity to have those thoughts," he turned back, "you will feel the urges building. However, you will have no means of satisfying any of them ever again. It will be quite unbearable, I can assure you."

Nick's anger grew as he gave up on his search and, for lack of any other action to take, he began walking behind Jeffrey again.

"You're enjoying this shit, aren't you!?"

Jeffrey fluttered his eyes and responded, still looking straight ahead, "Don't be silly. There's nothing to enjoy. That's the point. It doesn't thrill me to have to tell you any of this. In fact, all it achieves is to remind me of how bad every one of us has it down here." Jeff stopped and allowed Nick to catch back up, once again placing an arm around the young man's shoulders. "Now, please, try to control your anger. I mean, there's nothing you can do about it. What's gone is gone."

Jeffrey stopped, turned, and peered both forward and back as if having difficulty recalling which way they should be walking as he continued to speak over Nick's head. "So, as you're waiting for your pain cycle to begin again, keep in mind that while you're deep in thought, because that's really all you have here that you can call your own, you'll experience agonizing punishment in many other forms. You'll have pains from what once brought you pleasure that you'll have great difficulty dealing with. Oh, feel free to suffer in any way that you prefer. You know, yell, scream, sweat, grind your teeth, whatever. Just keep in mind, no matter what, the feelings won't go away. Well, that is, until your physical punishment arrives again to take your mind off other things. And, believe me, that will make you forget about all else through the duration." Jeffrey's signature smile returned with the latter statement as he looked down.

With Jeffrey still attempting to determine which direction to go, Nick's control over himself was now entirely lost. He shook himself free of Jeffrey's arm and yelled out, "You know what?! Screw you! And, screw whoever is in charge here too!" Nick was facing his host and pointing straight up into the man's face. "This is all just smoke and mirrors! I'm not buying any of it! And, you haven't proven anything to me! I haven't seen one thing in your little house of horrors down here that any of it is real!"

Jeffrey looked upwards and yawned before responding, "I believe you're missing something that was once between your legs the last time you checked. Isn't that real?"

Nick ignored the statement, not wanting to think about that, and looked around for another doorway to point out as he continued his tantrum. "It's pretty convenient, isn't it?! All the doors magically appearing when you want them to! And only tiny little windows that just you can see through!" Nick couldn't locate an actual door to use in his example, but he kept spouting, "Show me something! Show me anything! Anything that proves this place is real! Shit! For all I know this is some dungeon below the prison and you're just another guard having fun screwing with my brain after feeding me some type of hallucinogenic drug in my Jello pudding!"

Jeffrey formed a smiling frown and cocked his head, "Jello pudding? Hmmm." He glanced around as if attempting to locate someone famous before turning his head back to Nick and lowering his eyebrows, "A guard? Do you truly not recognize me?"

"I know who you are! Or at least who you look like! Big deal!"

Jeffrey remained with a calm voice, "Well if that's how you want to deal with the situation you're in, that's fine with me. I'm only trying to help you. It really is nothing to me if you choose to disbelieve what I'm telling you. It's alright, you certainly wouldn't be the first."

"Prove me wrong! Show me something!"

"My dear boy, this isn't a magic show. I can't just make something up for you. I can't simply pull a rabbit out of a hat just for you to see. Everything occurs repeatedly in the same order here. Nothing ever changes, except for the intensity. I can't simply open a door for you in hopes that the person on the other side is experiencing their cycle again. It just doesn't work that way."

"Bullshit! That's just bullshit! If Satan…"

"…Oh, dear…"

Nick hesitated only a moment before continuing, his voice echoing, "If Satan is really down here, then he can do whatever he wants! And, I want to see something right now! And, I want to see him! Not some errand boy sent to confuse me and get me lost in this maze!"

Jeffrey's voice remained monotone, "You really shouldn't…"

"Shut up! I've had enough! I'll say whatever I want!" Nick's finger remained in Jeffrey's face as he continued in his tirade, looking around as he yelled out, "Satan! Beelzebub! Lucifer! Mephistopheles! The Prince of Darkness! I can go on and on!"

Jeffrey raised one eyebrow while remaining consistently calm, "Well, you certainly are knowledgeable in your references to the master, I'll give you that. However, I'm afraid he isn't going to like that."

Before anything else could emit from Nick's mouth that was certain to make matters worse, he felt a slight tremor under his feet, and a sound similar to that of a rock avalanche coming from the wall behind him. Still pointing, Nick began to slowly turn his head. Jeffrey simply formed a slight smile and adjusted his glasses as he looked down at the young fool. As Nick's head turned to where he could see what was behind, he peered up to find a massive, double-digit scoreboard affixed to the walls. Boxed within the same type of ancient woodwork that the walls appeared to be constructed from was a display appearing as if it was made from faded, torn, and burnt parchment paper. There was a glowing from behind the parchment that illuminated the numbers, which showed two large double zeros. The anomaly briefly reminded Nick of an old flip-tile radio alarm clock he'd kept by his bedside as a teenager. The thunderous sounds intensified as the number on the right-hand side scrolled down ever-so-slowly to form a large '01' on the display. And, when the parchment stopped scrolling, it made an echoing explosion as if the avalanche had come to a rest. Dust fell to the floor from the bottom of the massive wooden frame and plumed when it landed, bouncing dust back up to the level of their knees.

Nick squinted as he watched and the sound pierced his eardrums. Upon the mechanism settling, Nick turned back to his host although remaining quite unamused, and equally unphased. He uttered sarcastically, "What was that?"

"I'm afraid he's not pleased with you. That would indicate that your punishment is to be intensified. And, so soon. Pity, really. Before you've even arrived at your room. It's been a while since I've seen that happen."

"Are you kidding me?" Nick reached and pointed behind himself, "So, that's supposed to be some sort of scoreboard that keeps track each time I break a rule?!"

Jeffrey perked up, impressed with Nick's observation, "Yes, exactly. Although, really, I'd rather not see that appear again. I mean, for your sake."

Nick's mockery reflected in his tone, "Oh, this is rich. A dark, smelly hallway that goes nowhere and a scoreboard that looks like it was built for the Roman Coliseum's chariot races. What's the matter, couldn't afford a newer, digital one?" The lights behind the parchment dimmed as the ominous monolith settled. Nick took notice, sarcastically smirking at Jeffrey, "Forget to pay the light bill?"

Jeffrey tilted his head and adjusted his glasses, "I'm very afraid that you're not understanding the significance of your situation, Nicholas. We're simply attempting to help you deal with, and understand, where you are and what's expected of you. If you don't want the help, there are others waiting who could certainly benefit from the information. It's your choice. It's always been your choice."

Part 5

Nick Goes on a Journey

As Jeffrey rubbed his eyes beneath his glasses, he asked his pupil, "I'm sorry, did you say something?"

"I said, how long is this walk going to take? My legs are getting tired." The statement was emitted with Nick's signature combination of sarcasm and annoyance as the two strolled along, side by side.

"I apologize. I couldn't quite hear you. The noises make it hard to hear through." Jeffrey shook his head as he glanced down, "Do you hear them?"

"I don't hear anything."

"Oh, dear. That's very unfortunate. Then I'm afraid it's nearly time again." Jeffrey looked back up and squinted from behind his darkened glasses as if a slight headache had come on. "I'm sorry, I didn't mean to make reference to the concept of what occurs in the now, and the not now, again. However, they're definitely getting louder, which means it's getting closer again."

"What's getting louder?"

"The screaming. Are you sure you can't hear them?"

Nick simply shook his head in response as he glanced up at his host and the two stopped walking. Jeffrey turned to face the younger man, "I'm afraid I may be required to excuse myself for a bit." Jeffrey winced as the noises within his head grew in intensity.

"What in the hell is your problem?"

Jeffrey managed to force an expression of annoyance through the ferocity of the screaming, as he did manage to overhear Nick's last comment. "Please, be careful. You're in enough trouble already," Jeffrey winced again and pinched the bridge of his nose under his glasses, shoving the rims upwards and closing both of his eyes tight. "And, to answer your inquiry, my cycle is approaching quickly. Are you certain you can't hear them?"

"Nope, nuthin."

Nick's attention was fully on Jeffrey. Primarily out of morbid curiosity in response to what was seemingly happening to him. It wasn't from fear, as Nick was becoming amused by what was apparently about to occur, and he wanted to watch. As he stared up at his host he could clearly make out that Jeffrey was perspiring and had a look forming on his face that, in Nick's opinion, reflected fear.

Jeffrey removed his glasses entirely and Nick saw tears beginning to stream down the man's face. Jeffrey opened his eyes and looked Nick straight in his while extending the hand that held his glasses. His host's eyes were severely bloodshot from the pressure of his fingers. "I don't suppose you would be kind enough to hold onto these for me?"

Nick looked at the glasses and simply took a step back, making no attempt to take the polite route and hold Jeffrey's eyewear.

Jeffrey's tone remained calm, "No, I thought not," as he folded the glasses and placed them into his shirt pocket.

Nick looked back up with a slight grin on his face, an obvious reflection of his evil-driven anticipation. He leaned in and saw through the low light that Jeffrey's eyes had closed again and his face was well water-stained. Nick also noticed that Jeffrey's knees had buckled and he was bent slightly forward and balancing himself with one hand on the dank walls of the corridor.

"I really must apologize," Jeffrey managed to moan before doubling over entirely, his voice cracking. As he did so the lights from the candelabra nearby seemed to dim, and many of the candles blew out entirely from a sudden warm breeze traveling through the hallway, causing the air to be heavier and even more uncomfortable than it had been. As the light faded lower, Jeffrey uttered a moan that reflected pain, *"Ungghhhh!"*

Nick's smirk remained, "What's happening to you?"

Jeffrey called out as he looked up from his knees, "Oh No! Please! *No!*"

Nick's eyes widened and although he couldn't see it, Jeffrey certainly could. The host looked up and viewed the heavy, braided rope as it was being placed down over his head. Nick watched intently and although the hangman's noose was invisible to him, what he did see was the imprint of the heavy, ancient cordage as it tightened around Jeffrey's neck, and the head of his host cocked to one side as the rope went taught. Nick's eyes grew even larger as he watched Jeffrey being hoisted by his neck straight up to the rafters above, and the man begin to choke violently. Nick could see no rope, no gallows, and no executioner. Nonetheless, he still assumed what Jeffrey was experiencing. He was also enjoying the display far too much.

With his head sideways from the tension, Jeffrey looked down to see what Nick was unable to view. The executioner was a large faceless man clothed poncho-style in torn rags and a hood. He had gray, stringy hair poking from his oversized arms, shoulders, and legs. On his feet were laced leather knee-high boots. He had just hoisted Jeffrey up and tied the ropes off to the hangman's platform. The servant removed from a scabbard tied to his waist a long, rusted serrated blade with a blood-stained wooden handle. He reared back and plunged the knife deep into Jeffrey's abdomen. His victim managed a muffled scream from beneath the choking of the rope. *"Unggghhhh!"*

Dark, red liquid flew from the blade as the executioner pulled it out violently, only to immediately drive it back in again.

"Aaaaarghhhh!"

Nick flinched to avoid getting hit with the warm fluid while watching the rips form in Jeffrey's clothing, and his host's clean pink dress shirt and jeans staining in the color of blood.

"Unnnggghhhh!" Jeffrey managed to moan through his state of asphyxiation, his bulging eyes looking down as he watched the blade penetrate deep into his stomach. He stared intently with fear as the executioner began to work the blade horizontally. Jeffrey could only emit a muffled cry as his larynx was being crushed by the thick, rough twine, and his body spasmed.

"Ummmphhhh!"

Nick stared as Jeffrey's body moved back and forth as the rough cut slowly formed across Jeffrey's stomach. The executioner, invisible to Nick, was moving the serrated machete with both hands in a sawing fashion, cutting through the flesh and tearing at the muscle. The blood flowed out freely and spilled down Jeffrey's pants, over his shoes, and splashed onto the wooden floor below. Nick's head and eyes followed the blood as it fell. He knew that Jeffrey was both here, and still not here, in that moment.

Nick looked up at the man who was being suspended three feet from the ground to see Jeffrey's eyes pleading with him. Although not actually looking at Nick, but rather through him. As for Jeffrey, he was now in an entirely different place far away and being suspended from the gallows. Nick felt that Jeffrey could still see him, and watched as the terrified man's puffy and bulging eyes begged for help that not only Nick couldn't provide, but was unwilling to. Nick gazed intently as Jeffrey attempted another scream only to have blood and mucous spew from his mouth and flow down his chin. The younger Nick took another step back to avoid being spat on, never once taking his eyes off the scene unfolding before him, and still with a truly evil grin on his face as if he were enjoying a good, gory horror movie.

As the blade reached the opposite side from where it began, Jeffrey lowered both of his flailing hands in an effort to catch his own intestines that Nick watched fall from the evisceration his host was experiencing. Jeffrey's attempts were futile as the blood-soaked, warm appendage slipped through his fingers and flopped down to the floor below. Leaving a trail of bowels that extended from his open stomach to the blood-soaked floorboards. The glowing from the cracks between the floor planking turned the maroon-colored blood a bright red as it seeped through the crevices.

Jeffrey's body began to flail again as the executioner turned the blade of the machete and began to saw down, slicing through his lower abdomen and down to his genitals. Nick frowned as he soon realized that Jeffrey's organs of pleasure had seemingly been returned to his body, at least temporarily. Only to be swiftly sliced off, and another muffled scream emitted as Jeffrey's organ dropped to the floor. As Nick watched the appendage splash among the blood and other entrails, he noticed the portion of Jeffrey's intestines that were dangling to the floor now began to rise back up. Nick looked up as Jeffrey's internal organ began ejecting from his backside. Nick couldn't see the second servant who was pulling his intestine back through the open wound and out of Jeffrey's anus in an apparent transanal evisceration.

Jeffrey's blood-soaked cries of pain couldn't be heard anymore as the vital fluids and phlegm that were drooling from his mouth, along with the choking of the rope, drowned out any further attempts to scream in anguish.

Once his colon had been entirely pulled back through his body and had again fallen to the floor, Nick watched as the invisible blade began to travel up the man's sternum. The executioner had both hands tight on the handle and seemed to struggle as Jeffrey's body spasmed from the pain, and his eyes continued to watch helplessly as the blade now dripping from his own body fluids and flesh, slowly approached his neck. Jeffrey's body could only twitch violently now, attempting to fight against the agony it was experiencing. Nick continued to gaze as the gaping hole in the man's torso widened from the flaying he was experiencing.

Jeffrey's eyes looked past the blade down to Nick and he found the strength to extend his arms in a desperate, silent pleading for the young man to help him in any way possible. Something that both Nick hadn't the ability, nor the desire to do as he'd backed himself fully against the opposite wall, and was leaning back with his hands tucked into his pants pockets. Nick's evil smirk remained as he seemed to be enjoying the gruesome site before him, truly wishing he had a box of popcorn to accompany this gory featurette. It was almost as if it wasn't real to Nick at all.

It was certainly agonizingly real to Jeffrey.

As the blade neared Jeffrey's neck, his arms dropped and dangled. Nick continued to watch as the hole in the man's chest gaped open wider, and the remainder of his gastrointestinal tract, his stomach, liver, and finally his heart all dropped to the floor. Each being severed from the muscles, nerves, and veins that held them inside Jeffrey's body. Each organ splashing in the river of blood now soaking the ancient woodwork below. Nick gazed as Jeffrey could do no more than cough up blood and spit, enduring every bit of the pain the executioner was causing, not having the ability to experience the luxury of death ever again or even to simply fall unconscious.

That just wasn't allowed down here.

◆ ◆ ◆

Nick didn't get to see the final moment when the executioner reached Jeffrey's neck and in one swift motion cut the man's throat from side to side just underneath the rope that was choking him.

Jeffrey himself watched while enduring the unimaginable suffering, as he did each time his body, or more so what was left of it, fell to the ground among the mess of entrails at the base of the gallows. And, as usual, his senses and eyesight remained sharp and focused as his body-less head swung on the rope and gazed down for a moment or two before it also dropped to the pile of remains below, bouncing on the platform, down the steep wooden stairs and into the flesh below it.

The reason Nick hadn't the ability to see the ending of Jeffrey's cycle of pain was that just before it occurred, Nick's eyes involuntarily blinked as they do for any normal person. When his eyes instinctively opened back up he found himself in another place, away from the dungeonous caverns, and away from the punishment that he'd been witnessing his host endure.

Nick looked at his surroundings and recognized himself as being in his room in his parent's house, standing in front of his own bedroom window. A confused Nick looked down at himself and even touched his body with both hands. He was in a bit of shock and didn't know how, or why he was there. He did, however, find himself to be fully intact again as his hands traveled up and down his midsection.

Nick looked back up and squinted through the sunlight that was shining through the glass. He twirled his body around to view his room, attempting to determine if what he was seeing was a mirage, or if he was truly there.

At first glance, Nick hadn't noticed the items lying on his bed. He looked all around, up and down, and came to the realization that he was, in fact, back in his own space within his parent's Florida home. A smile formed on his face as he again looked out the window to the front yard. He enjoyed the warm sunlight reflecting through, closing his eyes and soaking it in. He heard the sounds of the busy residential street outside as cars went by. He even took notice of birds chirping from the trees just outside his window. He opened his eyes back up, squinted, and gazed at the vapor trail of a jet going by high up in the sky.

Nick took a deep breath and recognized the familiar smell of his space, a combination of the detergent his mother used for the laundry and the foul odor of his dirty clothes. The same clothes that he always threw onto the rug and remained there until his mother would finally gather up and wash for him days later. His well-worn high-top sneakers thrown into the corner exemplified the odor floating through his bedroom. Nick was enjoying the feeling of comfort in being back in his own room.

Nick's smile faded when he turned around again and found the AR-15 assault rifle, the backpack, the body armor, ballistic vest, and the many rounds of ammunition stuffed into magazines lying across his unkept bed.

Nick spun back and looked down at the calendar he kept on his desk that sat in front of his window. He located the date, as all days before this one had a red 'X' marked through them. Nick realized that today was Tuesday, February 14th. Valentine's Day. His eyes darted to the electric, scrolling-tile clock beside the desk calendar, it was 12:01 p.m. Nick's head snapped up again, his eyes staring blankly through his thick glasses out of the window at the warm, sunny yard as a neighbor and their dog walked past on the sidewalk. Nick's mouth had gaped open, his eyes widened, and his thoughts raced. He quickly realized that he was back on the day that he'd committed his crime over eight years ago.

And, that it was nearing time to go.

Nick turned back to his bed and stared at the arsenal he knew he'd laid out. He knew that only minutes earlier, it had all been hidden away deep inside his closet where nobody would find it. He thought for a moment about how long it had taken to load all of the loose .223 caliber ammunition into the half-dozen or so magazines. He thought for a second about how much the tips of his fingers had ached after completing the task. He unconsciously glanced down as he rubbed the tips of the fingers on his right hand against his thumb. He looked over and also knew that there was an additional loaded handgun tucked inside the duffel bag. He knew it was there without even having to check for it.

Nick's eyes nearly crossed as he stared blankly at his bedroom walls and his memory went to the plan. He thought about how he'd determined that the best way to maximize the carnage would be to pull the fire alarm in the school's hallway and then simply wait for students to exit their classrooms. He knew he'd have no trouble mowing down dozens of students who each believed were evacuating their studies due to another mundane school fire drill. He knew that it would take precious time for any of the students to figure out what the noise from the assault rifle truly was, and they'd continue to enter the hallway even though their classmates would already be piling up dead on the floors. He thought that once they'd figured it out and no more were coming out, he'd begin his march up the halls, opening doors and shooting whoever was left until he ran out of ammunition, or his gun were to jam.

Nick thought about how he'd carefully planned out how it would all end. He'd determined that if he acted swiftly, and kept his head about him, he'd make it out of the school before the police arrived. He thought about how his plan didn't include shooting himself right away. Instead, he'd shed the vest and drop everything right there except for that one small .38 caliber handgun that he'd take with him to his favorite junk food restaurant just down the street from the school. There, he thought, he'd have one last burger, fries, and a soda before using the pistol on himself before anyone recognized him, and before the cops would arrive.

Nick smiled to himself as he continued to become lost in his thoughts. His memory began to justify the actions he was about to take and already taken once before when he was alive. He thought about how he felt he had earned the right to do what he was about to do. He was equally amused and amazed at the fact that nobody up to that point had taken notice, or any actions to stop him. Even after all of the gun-related purchases, social media posts, and personal comments to others. He thought about how he'd flagrantly displayed all of the warning signs and signals, and how nobody had taken him seriously.

He chuckled silently and said out loud to himself, "What a bunch of idiots." He thought of how society had failed in its attempts to protect innocent people and only succeeded in protecting the rights of those who seek to carry out violent crimes. He reflected on how monitoring a person's social media had now become an invasion of one's privacy, even for someone like him. And, if that had not been the case, he thought, the 'man' would certainly have figured it out and tried to stop him.

He thought of how easy it was for anyone, including himself, to obtain a gun. An automatic weapon no less, and how high-capacity magazines were considered 'normal' for the average person to own. He giggled at the thought of how in today's society those who are guilty are the victims, and the victims are now the guilty, and the ones that suffer the most.

Nick laughed out loud, shaking his head as he began to shove the weapons, the ammunition, and the body protection into the duffle bag. He couldn't imagine that Jeffrey, or whomever, was actually providing him another opportunity to carry out his plan for a second time. And, how he wasn't about to waste that chance. He then turned to look at the clock and watched as it scrolled to 12:02 p.m.

He glanced out his window again to the streetside to see if the cab he knew that he'd called about fifteen minutes ago had arrived yet to take him to the school. He chuckled again at the thought that some poor shmuck taxi driver was to become an unwilling and unknowing accomplice in that they were about to be his personal chauffeur to a school shooting. Nick noticed the cab pulling into the driveway, and he slung the duffle over his shoulder and trotted towards his bedroom door. A wide smile remained on his face.

He never hesitated.

Part 6

Asylums, Movies, Books and More Bad People

When Nick emerged from his bedroom door he found himself back in the uncomfortably warm, dank corridor. Gone from his shoulder was the duffle, and standing before him once again was Jeffrey. His host was dusting himself off as if particles of the earth were the only thing that had recently stained his clothing rather than his own blood and other body fluids. Jeffrey's clothes had returned to perfection, with no rips or tears from the blade that had traveled through his body, and no sign of the entrails that had fallen from it. His hair was perfect again and the only indication that he'd endured anything at all was his eyes, which were still puffy from the agonistic crying. And, neither the floor nor any of his surroundings now showed any sign of the torture that Nick had witnessed his host endure.

"Enjoy your little trip?" Jeffrey didn't bother to look up as he inquired, he simply continued to swat at his clothing.

Nick's anger once again returned, and again he stomped his feet like a child. "Dammit! What was that for, anyway, if you weren't going to let me finish what I'd started?! That wasn't fair! And, I for one don't appreciate it! Cut the bullshit, why don't you?!" Nick's demeanor changed slightly as he looked around and asked the next question with sarcasm, "Besides, I thought I wasn't allowed any more pleasure? If not, then why did I get sent back there to do it all over again?!"

"Well, first of all, it wasn't meant for you to enjoy. However, I'm certain the Boss will be pleased with the fact that's what you felt it was for. No, no, Nick. Think of it as more as having been a test. A test to see what you'd do when provided the same set of circumstances."

"A test?!" Nick's tone still containing sarcasm.

"Of course. As I said, I'm certain he's pleased with the results. Which, by the way, you failed."

Nick shook his head in disgust as he looked his host up and down, changing the subject, "Feeling better, are we? Tell me, was the pain intense? It certainly looked it." Nick's smile returned with his tone, "How did it feel when your balls fell to the floor?" Nick's face then turned to one of disappointment, rolling his eyes along with his head when he felt down and realized part of himself was once again missing.

Jeffrey finally looked back to his pupil, "That's a stupid question, now, isn't it? How do you think it felt?"

Nick attempted to work through his own disheartening realization that his manhood had been taken away for a second time. "By the way? Is the pain lingering? Do you still feel it after it's over?"

"I told you before, emotional and psychological anguish are a big part of the punishment. The physical pain subsides. What's left is the agonizing anticipation of when the next cycle will arrive again." Jeffrey completed his tidying by removing his glasses, breathing his hot breath on them, and wiping the lenses on his clean dress shirt before checking them for spots and placing them back on his nose. "Come now, there's still more to see and do."

"Just so you know, I don't regret what I did! And, I would have done it again!"

"Of course, Nick. I would expect no less from you." Jeffrey's signature grin returned with the statement as he placed an arm back around the shoulders of the younger man. "Come, now. As I said, much more to see and do." Jeffrey pointed ahead of himself as Nick looked up to see another corridor had formed in the distance ahead of them.

Jeffrey's voice showed signs of enthusiasm, "Ah, here we go. That corridor just up there, for instance. Many physicians and staff of various asylums are housed in that area."

"Okay, why?" Nick's tone was of complete defeat, as he now fully realized that they were back on their journey of hell's catacombs. Not to mention that only moments ago the newfound corridor hadn't been there and Nick was growing quite tired of things appearing…and disappearing.

Jeffrey looked a bit puzzled as he glanced down, "You're full of foolish questions, now aren't you?" He motioned to the corridor ahead as he continued, "Asylums during the 19th century were intensely cruel places. People just didn't know how to deal with mental illness. Not to mention, many of those held within the institutions weren't actually afflicted by mental illness. Many were simply victims of circumstance and made to endure archaic forms of what others believed to be legitimate medical procedures."

The two made their way towards the new passageway. Nick looked straight ahead and was overtaken with a feeling that the corridor they were approaching seemingly wasn't drawing nearer. He felt the more they walked towards it, the further away it became.

Jeffrey continued, "Just think, Nick if you'd lived in that time period, you could have been forced to live out your days at one of those places without having a legitimate medical diagnosis." He looked down and pointed to his pupil with his free hand, "Think about it, you could be given a diagnosis as simple as chronic laziness and be placed in a lunatic asylum. Why, some were placed in them for simply reading novels, for goodness sake. Can you just imagine that?"

"Reading books got you put in a crazy house?"

"Certainly. And, how mad is that to begin with? Epilepsy was a big one too, along with many other ridiculous reasons." Jeffrey raised a finger, "Ah, for being jealous of someone, that was one too. It was insane to begin with, placing people in places like that for reasons other than being legitimately ill. Oh! Being a wife that was deserted by her husband, or even a widower. Another silly reason. I mean, really, Nick. These people weren't crazy at all."

Nick looked up at Jeffrey as they continued to walk, "That's insane."

"Exactly. So, not only are those that condemned these poor people kept here, but also the physicians and staff that treated them so poorly, they're here too. Well, at the least the ones that knew better."

"What do you mean?" Nick continued to gaze down the hallway, wondering why the destination wasn't drawing nearer. This is too much like a movie cliché, he thought to himself.

"It's like I explained to you. If the physicians, nurses, and staff knew what they were doing was wrong, or deliberately mistreating the *patients*, a term I'll use loosely, then of course, they're here. If the caregivers, few and far between I might add, that were only doing as they were told and believed what they were going was truly helping the afflicted, then possibly not." Jeffrey looked at Nick, who was staring back up. "It's a fine line, that one."

Nick was taken aback when he turned his face as Jeffrey stopped, and they found themselves at the mouth of the corridor that seemed so far away to the young man just merely moments ago. Jeffrey directed them to turn at the opening of the new passageway and they both stared down the lonely, never-ending dark tunnel. Echoing through the darkness similarly to the last were the sounds of suffering, both loud and distant.

Jeffrey pointed, "Take that first door there." And, again, a doorway appeared for the young Nick to see. "That's Doctor Freeman's room. He experimented on those poor souls by means of performing unnecessary lobotomies on his patients. He'd take a metal pick and thrust it through the patient's eye socket, tap it through the skull bone with a hammer, and then twist it around in the frontal lobe of the brain. If his victim didn't die from cerebral hemorrhaging, they certainly didn't come out of it any better, nor were they cured of their particular ailment. If they even had one, to begin with."

Nick pushed his thick glasses back up his nose, "Yeah, okay, but again they thought they were helping those people, didn't they? I still say that the time period was to blame. Don't you think so?" Nick looked at his host with a snarky grin.

"Certainly not. We've discussed this already, Nicholas." Jeffrey pointed to another adjacent door. "In that room across is Doctor Burkhardt. He would drill into the patient's head with a hand drill and remove parts of their cerebral cortex, thinking he was removing the mental illness by removing part of the brain. Nasty results, I must say." Jeffrey looked down to his pupil, "Now, I ask you, regardless of the time period don't you think that's a bit barbaric? Not to mention, how is the Boss supposed to top that in terms of dishing out eternal punishments to the wicked ones? In fact, in case you hadn't noticed already, he creates many of the punishments just by simply modifying the cruel things that the human race has already come up with over the centuries to do to their own kind. It's kind of amusing if you think about it."

"So, you're telling me that *the Boss* has had no influence over humans at all and the cruel things they've invented to do to each other?"

"No, none."

Nick's disgust and skepticism remained, "Okay, fine. But I still say they were doing what they thought was right. I mean, this is what they did to treat people that they thought were ill. Was it their fault that the means were archaic because they didn't have modern medicines or know any better at the time?"

Jeffrey's look was one of befuddlement as he gazed down at the young lad. "Are you being serious, Nick? Treating someone with chronic laziness, or for simply reading a book, by drilling into their heads and removing parts of their brain? Or, even doing something like that to someone with an actual mental illness? Like that was ever a cure?"

Jeffrey removed his arm from around Nick's neck and placed a hand on his shoulder, "Let me ask you something. If someone had emphysema, would you cut their tongue out to make them stop coughing? Would you sew someone's mouth shut to cure them of the hiccups? Don't you think instead of trying to make a name for themselves and hastily performing barbaric surgeries they could have taken the time to theorize on the problem, determine if there in fact was an issue, and use more common sense in their treatment? Isn't that was an accurate diagnosis is meant to be?"

"Maybe. I don't know." Nick's tone reflected genuine disinterest. In fact, Jeffrey was surprised that Nick hadn't yawned when he inquired, "So, what do these two guys get?"

"Oh, well now, here's another exception to the rule when it comes to what they receive as a punishment. But, you seem bored with the conversation, so we should move on."

"Oh, come on! Let me see what goes on down there!" Pointing down the dark corridor, "Show me what they're experiencing!"

"No, no. We should move along. I'm sure you must have more questions, and our time is limited." Jeffrey closed his eyes and dropped his head. "Damn, I apologize. There I go again, making references to temporal measurement as if it had meaning here."

"Come on!" Nick was still facing the source of his anger, "Take me down that hallway and let me see what's going on!"

"Take you down what hallway, Nick?"

Nick spun back around to see the corridor that had been real to him mere seconds ago was now a solid wall once again. He looked up, down, and side to side. No entryways or doors to be found. He snapped back around to face Jeffrey, "Dammit! You're just screwing with me!"

Amused, "Well, that is the idea, now isn't it? I mean, isn't the point to cause you all sorts of anguish? Emotional along with the physical? It's all part of the plan. Haven't you noticed, my dear Nicholas, that along our little journey, you've displayed anger, frustration, and confusion? And fear?" Jeffrey's eyebrow cocked, "Sort of like how you left all those families to feel after killing their loved ones, now, wouldn't you say?"

"Screw you! And I *do not* fear anything!"

"Ah, yes, I expected no less than a reaction similar to that. Anyway, let's keep moving." Once again Jeffrey directed the upset young man and they continued to walk, seemingly in the direction they'd come from. With Jeffrey's arm once again around Nick's shoulders and his voice calm and poignant, he remarked, "By the way, Nick. If you truly haven't found fear in anything yet on our little journey, don't fret. You will."

♦ ♦ ♦

"Now, tell me, Nick. Do you enjoy movies?"

"Movies? Why are we talking about movies?"

"Just answer the question. Do you enjoy them?"

"Yeah, I guess so."

Jeffrey's head tilted up as they strolled, another display

of his conceit, "I'm particularly fond of *Angel Heart*." He glanced down, "Have you seen that one?"

"I don't think so."

"Ah, pity. It's a wonderful movie. Robert DeNiro plays my favorite character. You really should watch it sometime."

Nick's contempt for the comment was quite apparent, "You're real damn funny, aren't you! How am I supposed to watch a movie? Do you have a theater down here?!"

"True, my apologies. Still, it's too bad you've never seen that one. Oh, I'm also a fan of *Silence of the Lambs*."

"Now, that I can understand. There are certainly no surprises there."

"*The Infernal Cauldron* is another favorite. Tell me, my young Nicholas, what was your favorite movie?"

"I don't know. What does it matter?"

"It's just conversation."

"Fine. *Willie Wonka and the Chocolate Factory*. The boat in the tunnel scene."

Jeffrey squinted, staring straight as they kept a slow, but steady stride together in the tight corridor. "Interesting. I wouldn't have guessed that. What about books, Nick? Did you read? Do you know how to read?"

"Very funny! Of course, I do!" Nick stopped, and in a huff, "Aren't we walking in the same direction we came from?!"

Jeffrey begrudgingly glanced behind and forward, "I don't believe so. Why? Do you think we are?"

"I don't know." Nick's tone was back to defeat, staring behind himself.

Jeffrey continued to look around, "Well, I know we haven't gone past that room yet."

Nick looked back to see a doorway. Except, this time it wasn't closed, and it was a larger doorway than the others they'd encountered thus far. Two massive wooden doors, shaped to form a half-circle at the top were both open into a room beyond. Nick slowly crept to the doorway with

Jeffrey directly behind. When the young man stopped, he bent forward and peeked inside from the door's corner. What he saw left him in awe.

Before him was a room never-ending in size. There appeared to be no ceiling, nor a far wall, only what looked like the sky in the darkest of night, deep bluish-black in color that extended from overhead to the horizon. Nick believed he could make out distant stars in the sky and illuminating the darkness was a moon. Although primarily shadowed, appeared as if in its Waxing Crescent stage. It didn't exactly look to be the earth's moon as Nick recalled it being. Rather appearing to be the moon of some other planet in some other solar system.

The walls were not walls at all. But instead, endless stacks of literature in massive, antique bookcases with no end to them on the horizon. As he squinted and looked straight, at intervals in the distance at various heights appeared to be rope and planking catwalks that crossed from one side to the other. Each leading to narrow, thin walkways along each row of books. As Nick stepped into the room he found himself standing on a cobblestone pathway, maybe only ten feet wide which traveled between the bookcases and far reaching beyond what his sight had the ability to view. Blocking access to the bookcases to each side on the ground level was a wooden railing about waist high with no apparent breaks along it to access the books from the stone walkway.

Having crept just inside the door, Nick stood, staring. The odor he detected in this place was one of age, like old paper in a moldy, dank basement. Not surprisingly similar to being inside an old bookstore. The only light illuminating the room came from the bright sliver of the moon glowing from some distant sun elsewhere in this new universe. As he peered up, even though the sky had a moon and stars, the bookcases seemed as if they kept going and somewhere in the night sky they went far beyond the moon and enveloped the dark universe above, possibly touching each other at their highest point.

"What is this place?"

Jeffery came up behind his apprentice and again placed an arm around his shoulders. "It's his library."

"He reads?" The inquiry was delivered in a caustic tone.

"I didn't say he reads. But he does collect. You see, Nick, these are all the books that have ever been burned or banned throughout our history." Jeffrey corrected himself, "Well, all except for *that* book, of course. That one isn't allowed, for obvious reasons. But, all others are here. It's not difficult to locate a book that someone has desecrated, condemned, or simply refused to sell."

Nick took another step in and away from Jeffrey's grip and his head twisted and turned as he looked at all of the books that numbered into the infinite. For just a brief moment he also thought he saw the silhouette of someone, not really a man, but a creature, far off in the distance crossing slowly on one of the catwalks. The room seemingly had no end, it just faded into the dark skies above and into the distance ahead. The room had a more comfortable feeling to it than the corridors had felt to Nick.

"Can I look at one?" Nick placed his hands on the wooden railing and leaned in to make out a name on any of the novels. He flinched and yanked his hand back when he received another splinter for his efforts.

"No, Nick, you can't."

The young man turned his head and whined as he sucked on his splintered palm, "Then, why are you showing me this place? Why bother if I can't even look at one of them? Why didn't you just let me walk on past instead of having an open door to walk through?!"

"Because, Nick, showing you this place simply represents one more creature comfort you'll never experience again." Jeffrey stepped forward and returned his gentle grip on Nick's shoulder, "You're here for eternity, sitting and waiting for a cycle of pain and punishment to continually return. All you'll have while you're waiting will be your thoughts, nothing else. Wouldn't it have been nice to have a book to read to distract your mind from things you shouldn't be thinking about?" Jeff's other hand motioned to the room, "You will forever have the knowledge that there are thousands and thousands of books nearby. Banned and burned as they were, you can never read them. Not even one of them." Jeffrey's tone was teasing, "You might not think it matters right now, but just wait, Nick. The thought of this room will haunt you. Of that, I can promise."

Nick raised an eyebrow, his voice hinting disgust, "Do you really think that bothers me? That any of this bothers me?! Do you somehow think that I care?!" Nick spoke directly to Jeffrey while motioning to the library behind with his aching hand, "Do you think that I care about any of this? That I care whether or not one of his little henchmen is going to wheel a squeaky cart past my room and offer me a book or not? Well, I don't! Screw his book collection. And, while you're at it, screw you!"

In reality, Nick was lying about not caring, however, he didn't want his host to know differently.

Jeffrey winked and smiled. "Good to know, Nick." He lifted both eyebrows behind his dark glasses, "I sincerely hope you still feel that way after ten or twenty-thousand years." Jeffery shook his head, "Oh, dear. I apologize. There I go again with the reference to time."

Nick turned back and gazed at the books. "I said screw you! I've probably been here that long already!"

"*Hmmm.* Well, closer to seven hundred. But, who's counting? Come along, now."

Nick took one last look around before following Jeffrey, truly wishing he could take a book with him to read at a later time. He looked at his hand and also wished that he could see well enough to remove the splinters.

◆ ◆ ◆

"*Oh, oh, oh!* What about that bitch that killed her kid in Florida?!" Nick's inquiry was delivered with enthusiasm as he and Jeffrey continued their walk together, having left the library behind them and now back in the dark tunnels. The doors to the reading room had disappeared without Nick's knowledge as they strolled further away.

Nick continued, "You know, the one that partied and got all tattooed right after she wasted her kid? And then she claimed it was all her father or something once they found the kid's body!" Nick turned around to face his host, walking backward and pointing, "Or that babysitter crap that she made up and said that the nanny kidnapped the kid or something? You know, she lied about it for months while everyone was searching. She even took the cops to a place where she never worked. What was her name? You know who I'm talking about, don't you?"

"Yes, of course, I know. She's here with all the other child killers. Quite the overpopulated area too. It's very unfortunate to have to admit that."

"Now, she was truly evil!" Again, the smile and enthusiasm displayed by the young Nick troubled his host as he faced forward again.

"Well, you'd know about that, now wouldn't you?"

"Just tell me. What does she get?"

"Ah, yes, well, a very interesting case she is. The Boss took quite a liking to her from the get-go." Jeffrey glanced up and squinted behind his spectacles, "Now, let's see, if I recall, she is made to lie down strapped to a metal gurney while receiving a unique form of water torture." He glanced back down, "Instead of water, though, she looks straight up to see molten metal being dripped from a lead sprinkler. It strikes her face first. The intense heat slowly burning her skin further away from the point of impact with each drop, expertly avoiding her eyes, though. She must watch it all drop oh, so slowly. Well, that is, until it finishes with her face and finally does burn her corneas to the point she no longer has vision."

Jeffrey looked his younger protégé straight in his pupils and continued, "Once her eyes are gone, she must experience every unimaginably painful drop without having the ability to watch it coming, only to feel it burn when the liquid makes contact. Although, the torturer does move down rather slowly once the skin on her face has burned away to expose her nerves. He then continues to make certain the flesh on her entire body melts away while she agonizes, fully conscious, and unable to rise from the table." Jeffrey raised a hand and pointed, "Oh, and the irony being the figure that stands above her, shaking the sprinkler at intervals to drip the burning liquid? He's made to resemble her father. Not that she sees much of him once her optic nerves have charred to the point of the loss of eyesight, mind you. But, it is rather amusing before that happens."

"Ouch."

"Yes, exactly. However, she's one of those that couldn't play by the rules here, either. Much was the case when she was alive. So, once the dripping liquid finally takes her last little toe, she still isn't done, as it was when she first arrived. There have been a few enhancements since then." Jeffrey placed a hand to his mouth, looked to the floor, and shook his head, "Only then is her body, down to only muscle, veins, and bone, placed in a vat of hydrochloric acid." Jeffrey smiled and raised both eyebrows, "A particularly favorite chemical of mine, by the way." Jeffery looked back straight and motioned with a hand, "At that moment, her remaining nerves feel her own body dissolve, painfully slowly. Of course, with her tongue having been blistered away in the early stages there's no chance of her screaming while it occurs. Although, she does try." Jeffrey chuckled, "Which is good, I suppose. She is quite the screamer before the articulators have melted."

"That's rough."

"So, you see, Nick, it is quite important that you play by the rules while on our little journey and beyond. If not, it can become so much worse for you. I mean, the pain is bad enough already. Why make it worse for yourself?"

"If you say so."

"Ah, here we are," Jeffrey uttered with slight enthusiasm as the two arrived at a crossroads in the corridor. Again, the intersection arriving without warning and taking the young Nicholas by surprise. "Speaking of familicide."

The two stood at the junction with the passageways going both left and right, and also continuing forward. Even in the flickering candlelight, the darkness of the hallways made it impossible for Nick to see an end in any direction. And again, no immediate doorways were within view.

Jeff stood at the crossroads, looking both ways. "I do believe we've arrived at the area where the familicides are kept."

"Familicide? What's that?"

Speaking above the younger man's head as he looked around, "The ones that commit crimes against their own families. Please, Nick, try to do better. That was an easy one."

Nick blew off Jeffrey's comment with a foul expression.

"I'm surprised you've never heard of them. Unfortunately, another crowded section of our little slice of…" Jeff frowned down at Nick, "Okay, that would have been a poor metaphor. My apologies. Anyway, there's quite a population of them here. Those that cause intense harm or kill their siblings are a nasty breed. Just think, Nick, the murdering of one's own parent, or parents. That's a metaphor within itself, don't you think? In essence, killing a part of yourself by doing away with the person that created you."

"I don't think so." Nick disregarded the deeper meaning as he leaned forward and gazed down the dank corridors.

"Of course, there are exceptions to the rule, as there always are."

"What do you mean?"

"Well, if one kills out of self-preservation, let's say. You know, a wife kills her abusive husband, for instance, before he kills her first. Or a child takes the life of an abusive parent. No, those ones aren't here. These are the ones that kill out of the usual excuses. You know, anger, greed, those sort of things.

"So, they only end up here if they killed someone, right?"

Jeffrey turned to face his pupil again, and his frustration was apparent, "You really haven't been listening, have you, Nicholas? The simple question itself reflects your immaturity and lack of intellect. Of course not. Do you really think that those who physically abuse children, or their significant others, don't end up here? That somehow simply because a death isn't involved that their actions are justified, and ultimately forgiven? That somehow it was okay?! Don't be ridiculous!"

Nick stared with disinterest.

Jeffrey calmed himself, "Do you really believe that a wife who is beaten by her husband on a regular basis and doesn't know when the next time it will occur again, or what the severity will be, or what the trigger will be, that she doesn't experience just as much mental pain and anguish as the physical?" His host shook his head, "No, no, Nick. Those who display cowardly acts of violence such as inflicting constant physical and emotional pain on a woman, lover, or a child, come straight here. They don't deserve to be absolved, nor do they deserve to be placed in the middle plain to be allowed to ponder their ways. There's simply no chance that they'll ever get to the top floor. They committed conscious actions and made their decisions. In turn, we've made ours."

Jeffrey sighed heavily, "I've tried to explain to you, Nicholas, that the emotional pain is just as important as the physical here. It matters just as much. Did my former explanation of how an abuser is likely to be treated not find its mark in you? Does it not occur to you that the similarities between the battered spouse, and everyone that's down here now, are in fact treated the same? This is important, Nicholas. You must pay attention. Just like the battered wife, you will not know when your physical pain will begin, how intense it will be, or what you might do to trigger it next. Or what you might do, quite unintentionally I might add, to make it even worse. Think about it. You are now that battered spouse, Nicholas. The only difference being, that you will never escape from it."

"Whatever." Nick glanced around, ignoring the warning, "So, tell me who's here? Name somebody."

Jeffrey's disappointment displayed, and with another heavy sigh, "Oh, there are many, Nicholas, I'm quite sorry to say. Like that door over there on the left."

"I wish you'd stop doing that," Nick mentioned as again when he looked to where Jeffrey was motioning in the newly discovered hallway there was, in fact, another door that had appeared.

Jeffrey replied sarcastically, "I didn't realize I was doing anything. Anyway, in that room is that famous football player that murdered his estranged wife and her male acquaintance. I'm certain that you're familiar."

"I know who you mean. Didn't he get away with that? He was found to be innocent, wasn't he?"

"Only in life, Nick. Certainly not in death. You can't fool the Boss, or the big man, either. You can only fool the foolish jury." The two approached the door together, with Jeffrey peering through the tiny window. "That certainly was the problem with the justice system during your time, now wasn't it my young Nick? Too many technicalities. Too many ways the guilty person could be found innocent. Even though society knew well and better." Jeff looked down, "In fact, what good is a justice system that doesn't deliver justice at all? One little slip of the tongue, one little smudge at a crime scene, one little piece of evidence mishandled in an otherwise undeniable case? One change of a hairstyle or a ridiculous display of a hand garment. What good is it, Nick? A lot of time and resources wasted, that's what." Jeffrey stared back through the glass-less window. "That's why this place is so important. The glove doesn't have to fit down here, my dear Nicholas. We use a bit more common sense in delivering justice, and in handing out punishments."

"So, what happens to him?"

Still gazing through the tiny opening, Jeffrey responded quite nonchalantly, "He gets a football shoved up his ass repeatedly." He then looked at his young walking partner and winked, along with a smirk.

Nick frowned, "What? You're kidding, right?"

Jeffrey cracked a big smile, followed by a hearty laugh. "Oh, come now, Nick. Have a sense of humor, why don't you? Of course not." The two began to stroll away from the door with Jeffrey leading. "Although the visual that I provided wasn't very far from the truth. You see, Nick, in reality, he receives a form of the guided cradle. Of course, there is another name for it that we don't use down here."

"What's a guided cradle?"

Jeffrey pointed into the air, "Ah, yes. Again, we have the Spaniards to thank for inventing that one. Now, let's see, how can I explain this to you so that you'll understand?" Jeff pointed the finger at Nick, "Ah! Think of a wooden barstool. Only, where the seat should be, there is a large triangular-shaped piece of wood, the point obviously sticking straight up. Now, our friend is suspended, unclothed of course, high above the device with his arms bound behind. To either side are the executioners, each holding a rope that extends to both of his ankles. Also dangling from his ankles are chained weights." Jeffrey's voice was loud, proudly explaining the device of pain, "Balls of steel to be exact! With another one being chained around his neck, all for the purposes of weighing him down, of course. He's then slowly lowered as the headsmen pull his legs apart using the ropes and, as you can well visualize, the point of the triangle slowly penetrates and…" Jeffrey stopped himself, looked down, and in a lower voice, "Well, you can probably picture the rest, can't you?"

Nick winced at the thought.

"Once the point finds its way to his stomach area, let's

just say agonizingly slowly, the headsman on his left chops his head off just above the chain with a battle ax. His head rolls onto the floor so that he can continue to watch. And certainly, no less, he still experiences the sensation of his body continuing to be impaled on the device. Just a bit of irony and humiliation, as it were. You know, having to watch a long pole traveling through your own body like a shishkabob." Jeffrey's eager description struck its mark as Nick was frowning. "His screams of pain are quite deafening. Well, that is of course, until his vocal cords are severed when his body loses its head. But the anguish still lingers between the receptors in his brain and body. The synaptic gap takes on all new meaning there, I can tell you."

Nick felt an uneasy feeling while staring up at his host. Not being certain as to whether it was Jeffrey's unique description, or whether or not he was still experiencing the disturbing sensation that the halls were continuing to gently sway.

Jeffrey looked up and down the corridor. "Now, let's see. Which way to go? I suppose forward is best, especially seeing that there's no going back."

Nick looked back to the intersection that was there just moments ago. It was now gone again, only to be replaced with a dimly lit corridor behind them with only darkness where the end might somewhere be. When he returned forward, he saw another door to his right.

"Now, here we have an interesting one. Quite famous for his time, in a sense. Although more people tend to recognize what was alleged to occur after his death, rather than during his life." Jeff approached and peered through the opening in the door. "Here we have Ronald."

"I don't suppose I could have a stepstool or something?!"

Jeffrey didn't bother to look away from the window when he commented in monotone, "No, you can't."

"Fine. So who is Ronald?"

"Oh, come now, Nick. You must have heard of him. I

mean, movies were made about his story. Books, documentaries. Paranormal investigators have studied his case. I told you, he's quite famous." Jeff now looked down at his student. "Not like you." The quip was accompanied with a wide smile and sarcasm.

"I really don't like you." One of the more serious, but snarky comments to be made by Nick.

Jeffrey's focus returned to the door's window and his signature smile was present, "I'm not here for you to like, Nick. Anyway, Ronald here killed his father, mother, two sisters, and two brothers. His entire family. He then claimed voices told him to do it." Jeffrey glanced down "Again, a cowardly excuse if you ask me. After claiming the voices commanded him, false claims I might add, people began to believe that the house he committed the murders in was haunted."

Nick's nerves caused him to jump when a terribly loud scream thundered from the other side of the door. Many more of the same from within the room from someone experiencing intense pain followed, and the wailing began to rise in tone rather quickly. Nick stretched his neck out again and tried desperately to see past his host inside the room to no avail. He simply wasn't tall enough. The shrieking intensified, as did the pitch until the final cry had risen like an acoustic guitarist strumming the high E string and moving a finger along the string to the sound hole, reaching the highest pitch manageable before letting off the string. The sound pierced Nick's ears as he held his hands over them and his face contorted.

Jeffrey's demeanor remained constant. He remarked quite casually as he continued to watch through the opening as the wailing stopped abruptly with a loud crunching sound, "Well, that was good timing, wasn't it?" Jeffrey dropped his head, "My goodness, I must apologize once again. It seems we're continually making reference to that which doesn't exist anymore, now aren't we?" Jeffrey peered back through the opening and said jokingly, "I'm blaming you. You started it when you first arrived and mentioned the concept of time."

Nick was ignoring Jeffrey's words. "What's happening in there?! It seemed like it didn't last long at all!"

"Oh, they're not done with him. He simply can't scream anymore." Jeffrey glanced down at Nick. "The demons ripped his lower jaw off." He peered back through the window and sighed heavily, "Probably not the only thing that will be torn from his body before they're through with him."

As Nick continued in his attempt to get a look into the room, which wasn't to be achieved, Jeffery simply turned away and began to walk. "Come along, now. Still more to see and do."

Nick continued to hear a crunching noise, now accompanied by a cackling laughter, although not human sounding. "What's going on in there?!"

Jeffrey stopped, glanced back, and replied, "Oh, nothing really. Just the hyenas. At least I think they're hyenas. Whatever they are, they're very hungry." He glanced down at his pupil again. "Come on, let's keep moving."

Nick stared back at the door as his host tugged on his shirt sleeve to keep him moving. Nick very much felt a need to see what was occurring in that room.

Part 7

The Empty Room

It was apparent that Nick was growing weary, as he'd begun to display a tired limp in his right leg that hadn't gone unnoticed by his host. Nick tried to ignore his gait and pain. "So, what's the deal with ghosts?"

"Ghosts?"

"Yeah, ghosts. You know, spooks and spirits. You mentioned the last guy's house was part of a ghost story. So, are they real? Why do some dead people still roam the earth?"

Jeffrey's puzzled expression also reflected his sincere interest in the question. *"Hmmm.* Okay, I suppose we can discuss that. But, only because it relates to the middle plain. And, I so enjoy stimulating conversation. Let's take a break and talk about it, shall we?"

"Take a break? Where?"

Jeff looked over Nick's head, as the two had stopped walking again and were facing each other. "How about that room right behind you? I do believe it's empty."

Nick turned to see a doorway behind himself. He turned back with a look of annoyance on his face. "I really don't like it when you do that."

"Do what? Come now, I think that space will do." Jeff reached past his young apprentice and took hold of the long, wooden handle. This particular door, although identical to all the others except for the library, had no lock or chain attached. Jeffrey pushed the large door open slowly and it creaked on its old, rusted hinges. He poked his head inside the dark room, "Yes, this will do." He then backed up, extending his hand to offer the room to his young acquaintance.

Nick leaned inside the doorway and reared back, turning his head to look up at his host, "Why isn't this room taken? Was there someone here once?"

Jeffrey smiled, "Of course not. Once you're here, you're here forever. We don't lose anyone or shuffle them around. It's simply empty and waiting for a soul to fill it. Please, step inside." Jeffrey realized the concern, "Don't worry, it's not yours. We won't be here too long. Just a rest stop on our journey, that's all. I promise."

Nick hesitantly stepped into the room and took his first look. It didn't surprise him that it was small, maybe twelve-by-twelve, and made up of the same dark-stained and deeply aged woodwork that everything else was. One single chandelier hung from the rafters in the center, full of hundreds of burning white candles. In the center of the room was a rectangular table of the same thick, ancient lumber. It was relatively small and to either side were two short, wooden bench seats. Nick was convinced that if this place wasn't hell, then it must be the depths of an old galleon ship that he was forever riding on relatively calm seas. And, he desperately wanted to go topside and feel the warmth of the sun and ocean breeze on his face rather than the airless, uncomfortable heat surrounding him where he was now.

Jeffrey walked past and stood at the table, motioning for Nick to sit and face him. Nick remained nearer the doorway with a dubious look on his face.

"You're telling me that if I sit down, this door behind

me isn't going to close forever, or just disappear completely?"

"Of course not. I told you, this isn't your room. It's just a place to rest and hold a nice little conversation. Don't worry, the occupant of this room isn't due to arrive quite yet, we won't be disturbed." Jeffrey's expression turned to concern, "Unless, of course, you don't want to. Maybe you just want to get to your space and forget about all the walk and talk? Possibly you're growing tired of the company? Although, one would think you'd take full advantage of the conversation before you forever have no one to talk to."

Reluctantly, Nick parked himself opposite his host as he continued to study the room. He noticed again that he couldn't make out any ceiling in the darkness above the candles. He felt very uneasy inside this space, not knowing what might jump out at him or crawl up his leg. He also very much believed that the door was going to close, so he chose the side facing the exit just in case he needed to make a quick move.

Jeffrey took notice. "Would it make you feel better if we were to put something in the doorjamb so it doesn't close?" Jeffrey looked around the floor as if he were going to locate a stopper, speaking with a demeaning tone as if poking fun at Nick.

"I'm fine. Forget it. So, this is what I'm going to be stuck in for the rest of my life?"

"Nicholas, you're already dead. There's no life left to live. Your life ended when the joy juice hit your veins. And, to answer your inquiry, yes. This is basically what your room will look like to you when you're not in your cycle. Why? Does it not suit you? Too early, perhaps? I can tell it makes you feel uncomfortable to be here. Maybe you'd rather have our conversation somewhere else?"

"Anywhere else."

"Yes, well, wouldn't we all like to have something that we can't have? But I'm sorry to say that it must take place here. You see, here is all you have now. There are no more blue skies for you, nor gray ones. You'll never see or speak to another human again. You'll never even utter any words. Your mouth will open only to scream out in pain."

Jeffrey's voice turned stern as he leaned forward, tilted his head down just a bit, and peered out over his glasses, scowling at the younger man. "That's so important to him, that you never again experience pleasure of any kind. Only pain. No sensations, other than anguish and sadness. No laughter, only crying. You'll never experience a bird singing, a dog barking, or even the simple comfort of the stridulation of grasshoppers on a warm summer's night. All things that you'll long for so terribly, and once took for granted. However, you'll never enjoy again." Jeffrey's smirk returned, "You'll never have an orgasm, or even feel the soft kiss of a woman." A sarcastic expression overtook his host, "Speaking of that. Have you ever had an orgasm with a woman, Nick? Or, was it always self-abuse? Or, possibly your cherry was popped in prison?"

Nick's eyes widened and he opened his mouth to angrily respond.

Jeffrey cut him off with a wave of his hand, "Never mind. It doesn't matter anymore." Jeffrey sat back and his voice turned somber, "It won't be so bad, though. You'll get used to it. I mean, what choice do you have? None, really. Now, questions. You must have questions."

Nick's demeanor remained unchanged, "*Hmph*. Sounds like I'll just sit there and go mad."

Jeffrey smiled an evil, wide smile and leaned in again. His voice was soft and monotone, "Mad? *Mad?* Do you really think he'd let you escape your pain by allowing you to go mad?" Jeff leaned back again, "No, I'm sorry to say, you won't be granted that luxury. You'll remain quite sane, and fully aware at all times. In fact, your mind will be sharper than it's ever been. Believe me, he will make certain that your nerves and senses are detailing every experience that you'll be forced to endure here. Going mad simply isn't an option, nor a way out." Jeffrey motioned casually with his hand, "Although you'll want to. You might even beg to go mad, who knows? But he won't let you. Oh, and just so you know, he despises begging. He sees that as a weakness, which is what it truly is at the core, don't you think?" Jeff removed his glasses, holding them up to the candlelight in an effort to check for dust, "He expects it, though. The begging. And, you will beg, when you're not simply crying out from the pain itself." Jeff was satisfied his lenses were clear and rested them back on the bridge of his nose. "You'll beg, you'll plead, you'll offer anything to make it all stop. But, alas, there's nothing left to bargain with, Nick, and it will all fall on deaf ears." Jeffrey poked his own temple, "So, try your best just to keep it in here. That's good advice."

"So, there's nothing I can do about it? Nothing. No mercy or anything. That's what you're saying?"

Jeffrey's expression returned to one of concern. "Mercy? Mercy for what? My goodness, Nicholas, you can't be serious. Your chance for that has long passed." Jeff pointed, "You decided your fate long, long ago. Not to mention, you had every opportunity to simply not do what you did. Those were your choices."

Nick pointed back at his mentor, "Hey! I did it because of the way I was treated! They had it…"

Jeffrey leaned in again and cut the young man off, "They had what? Had it coming? Is that *really* what you were going to say? Please!" Jeff leaned back further and regained composure. "Well, there you go, blaming society again." He threw his arms in the air, "It was never your fault, was it, Nick? Hey, everyone, look at me and see what society did to me." Jeff put his arms down, rested his elbows on the table, and pointed with one hand. "I've got news for you, it was nobody's fault other than your own. It doesn't matter if you're parents ignored you. It doesn't matter if other kids picked on you. It doesn't matter whether or not you grew up in poverty, or if you were rich. You decided how you were going to deal with life. Nobody made that choice for you."

"Whatever."

"Think about it, Nick. You had two basic choices. The same choices anyone in your situation before, or after you had. You hated the way life and others were treating you, so you decided to take matters into your own hands. You grabbed a gun and murdered fifteen children and two adults." Jeffrey cocked one eyebrow and tilted his head, speaking as if he were talking to a small child, "Did it ever occur to you that you could have chosen what was behind curtain number two? Did it ever cross your tiny, little mind that you could have done what so many others in your situation have chosen to do? That you could have grown up and made something of yourself? Even something great?"

Jeffrey lounged backward as if he was seated in a high back chair that wasn't visibly there. "And, if so, you could have returned, let's say to maybe a high-school reunion years later, and actually shown them what a success you had become. Wouldn't that have been the ultimate punishment for them? To show the prom queen turned prostitute or the sports jock who grew up selling used cars, what greatness you'd become? What a more successful person you turned out to be in comparison to them? Wouldn't it have been far better to make them live with *that* reality rather than what you made those families go through, and what you forced them to live with?

Nick simply stared, slightly frowning at his host with contempt. His anger churned in the pit of his stomach once again.

"But no," Jeffrey shook his head slowly and lowered his brow. "Instead you took the easy, and cowardly way out. Instead of being patient and taking the time to make something of yourself, you decided to waste five minutes and kill seventeen people instead.

Nick snapped a finger up, "Okay, hotshot! What about you?! You didn't come out of this any better than me, now did you?!"

A smile washed across Jeffrey's face. "I never said that I

was any different. Oh, don't get me wrong. I'm certainly better than you, to that there's no doubt."

"Bullshit! You're just as bad! Just because it took you longer to kill your victims doesn't make you any better than me!" Nick's eyes widened and the pitch of his voice raised an octave, or two, and he extended his arms, "Come to think of it, your worse! You didn't just kill people, you tortured and ate them if I remember correctly!" Nick's tone amplified with sarcasm and he pointed, "At least I didn't get hungry when I was doing it! You're just disgusting!" Nick squinted behind his thick glasses, closing one eye and lowering his tone, "You should get so much worse than me down here! Your body should've been boiled in acid after you were cut open, just like you did to your victims! Or a hole drilled through your skull! Remember that one?!"

Jeffrey smiled again, "Why Nick? I'm humbled that you recall my achievements." His tone turned sarcastically sincere, "I feel so honored that you remember. I may actually shed a tear."

"Oh, cut the crap, you sicko!"

Jeff's demeanor turned back serious and his tone to one of reasoning, "This isn't a competition, Nick. It's not about whose crimes were worse. It doesn't matter. We're here in this place, that's what matters. In the grand scheme of things, we're equals along with every other piece of garbage down here. The point is, we chose our destinies, and we continue to do so. I told you before, it can't get any better for you, but it can certainly become so much worse."

Nick slumped and sighed heavily, "If you say so."

"Let's face it, Nick, we didn't make the best use of our time. And now time doesn't even matter. If we'd only known then what we know now, eh, Nick? Now, let's not waste this opportunity by quibbling over who's the better person. Neither one of us are. That's why we're here."

"Fine"

"Let's see now, what were we discussing?" Jeffrey looked up and squinted. "Ah, yes! Ghosts, wasn't it? And, how their bodies are in purgatory."

"Purgatory?"

"Yes, of course. You see, the ones still wandering around among the living are the souls of those waiting in purgatory. Only the body and mind are waiting there, left alone to deal with their thoughts and their decisions. Their souls are left on earth while they're in wait. Stuck there, you might say."

Nick's anger washed for the moment as he carried on the conversation with his host. "Is that why they're so angry? I mean, I watched those paranormal television shows. The ghosts are always scaring people and throwing things."

Jeffrey uttered a heavy sigh, "Don't be stupid, Nicholas. Coincidence and mice inside the walls, that's all those television shows ever were. Do you really think the rules would allow someone who's in wait to have their soul caught on camera? No, only in secrecy do the living ever experience a true haunting of those waiting for their judgment." Jeffrey's tone remained pompous, "Just like the rumor that children were ghosts on those ludicrous paranormal shows. Do you really think the big man on the top floor would allow a child to be caught in the land of the undead? That's just silly."

"So, the whole thing about residual hauntings? Poltergeists? All of that?"

"They're all the same. Just a soul that doesn't understand why they're wandering. Not until the decisions are made by the mind elsewhere. They're just simply in limbo, and from time to time, they show themselves. Their energy builds to a boiling point. And then they knock over a teacup or throw a small rock or something. That's all it is."

"Well, what about demons? Do they exist? Are they influencing the living? You know, are they making people do bad things?"

"Do you think that's what happened to you?"

"No."

"Well then, there's your answer. Nobody forced you to

do what you did. No unseen entity guided you to pull the trigger, or planted the thought in your head, to begin with. You did that all on your own." Jeffrey's voice turned sarcastic again, "You watched too many horror movies, Nick. Demons only exist down here to do the master's bidding."

"So, you're saying that neither the big guy or the Boss has any influence on what a person does while they're alive, or how they act?"

"Of course not." Jeffrey sighed again, still reclining in his invisible chair. "Think of it this way. Life itself is a test. A test to see what you'll do, good things or evil things. Or, maybe you just go along for the ride. Regardless, once you've passed, only then does the management decide what happens to you, and where you ultimately end up." Jeffrey leaned to face his apprentice once again, "You know something, Nick? These are the first intelligent questions you've asked so far. I'm impressed, my young friend."

"Whatever. I'm not your friend. I'm not here to impress you, either."

"Quite obviously. Now, more questions. You must have more questions."

"Not really." Nick began to look around the tight space again.

"Oh, come now. Don't let this opportunity pass you by. Eternity is a long time to have no one to talk to. You must have more questions about this place, or about topics we're limited to talking about." Jeffrey shook his head again, "Oh, goodness. I mentioned time again. I really must stop doing that. I don't want to confuse you. I'm going to have you believing in the concept of orbital periods if I keep it up. I do apologize."

Nick glared and shook his head slowly at his host.

Jeffrey then perked up and sat straight. "Oh! By the way, speaking of time." He whispered, "Which we really shouldn't." His voice returned and he remarked proudly, "Did you know that it's believed that time itself has a relationship with the concept of reincarnation? That, under the philosophy of temporal finitism it's believed that there are repeating ages over the lifespan of the universe. And, that this leads to the belief that the earth experiences cycles of rebirth and reincarnation." Jeffrey sat back again and Nick thought for a moment that he truly heard the leather of a soft lounge chair make a noise when Jeffrey reclined.

His host continued in his signature pompous tone, "Don't you think that's interesting? Although, completely untrue. I mean, you and I are here, aren't we? We haven't been reborn as someone else. At least, as far as we know."

Nicholas could feel a slight headache coming on as a result of the conversation.

"Just think, Nick. What if that were true?" Jeffrey perked up again and sat straight. "What if your soul has two parts? A good side and an evil side. What if the garbage ended up here and there's another part of you that went on to be someone else? And, the shitty part of you down here never knows anything about it?" Jeffrey reclined again, his lips forming a wide smile, "What do you think, Nick? Was there any good in you that's now living a new, better life somewhere else, and the trash sitting before me is just stuck down here for all eternity?"

Nick squinted. "You're an asshole."

"Ah, maybe. Anyway, we shouldn't talk about things that have no meaning to your existence now. So, more questions?" Jeffrey perked up again, "Oh, I have one. What about fear, Nick? You must have fears? You know, things that caused you to hide under your blanket as a child and kept the light in your bedroom closet turned on at night? Possibly snakes? Or maybe spiders? You know, things you'd rather not have crawling out of your crevices during your cycles of pain."

Nick was snarky, "Yeah, like I'm going to tell you that. Just so you can tell the Boss and then it's used against me down here!"

Jeffrey leaned back again and Nick for certain heard the

leather cushions squeak. "I'm fairly certain he already knows your deepest fears, Nick. Now, more questions?"

Angrily, with a violent shaking of his head, "Fine! What about exorcisms? Are people really possessed by demons?"

"*Hmmm.* Now, that's a good one. Not to mention, you should already know the answer to that."

"How in hell would I know?" Nick closed his eyes, noticing his slip of the tongue all too late.

Jeffrey closed his eyes and sighed, speaking with defeat in his tone, "Oh, dear. That's unfortunate. I'm afraid you've done it again."

"*What?*" Nick's saucy attitude quickly turned to one of caution as the table began to shake, along with the chandelier above shimmering as dust fell from the rafters, pluming on the tabletop as it landed. The familiar low thundering sounds returned, growing louder as Nick noticed Jeffrey look up behind the young man. Nick's head snapped around and discovered that the large counter had appeared once again. Nick clamped his hands over his ears as Jeffery sat eerily still and they both watched as the faded and burnt parchment counter scrolled downwards from '02' to '03' with a loud explosion that ended with the entire room shaking.

When the dust settled and the rumbling subsided, Nick turned back around to see Jeffrey blankly staring back at him. As Nick lowered his hands from his ears, Jeffery crossed his arms and watched as the last of the dust dropped down in front of his face. Casually, Jeffrey spoke, "You just can't help yourself, can you?"

Nick threw up his arms and blurted quite disrespectfully, "So, what?! Now I've made it even worse?! And, what's the deal with the *three*?! The last time that thing showed up it was only on one!" As the question was asked, the scoreboard faded away without the younger man's knowledge.

"Think hard, Nick. You might just figure that out on your own."

"And how am I supposed to know how much worse I've made it all?! I don't even know what I was starting with! How could I possibly realize that it's gotten worse before it's even begun?!"

"Oh, you'll know."

"How?!"

"I told you, Nick. Once you arrive you'll see it happen to you, just once. Like a movie. You'll see what it was set to be when it all began." Jeffrey leaned in again and the invisible cushions squeaked, "And then, once the pain finally does arrive in the physical sense, and it's worse than what you thought it was to be? Then, you'll realize what you could have had, and what you've caused yourself through no actions other than your own inability to play by the rules." Jeffrey leaned back, "Now, let's get back to the topic. And, please. Try to control yourself."

"Fine." Nick was defeated again, sighing heavily. He then glanced behind and discovered to no surprise that the anomaly had disappeared. He turned back, slowly shaking his aching head.

"Exorcisms was it not? Now, Nick, think about it. These are the stuff of fantasy, don't you agree? I mean, let's say someone has a true mental illness. Schizophrenia, for example. And, they act in a way that others can't understand or explain. So, they call in a priest to *exorcise* the demons out, rather than turn to modern medicine to treat the illness."

Jeffrey removed his glasses and placed them on the tabletop, rubbing his eyes as if in an attempt to wipe away a headache of his own. "Oh, sure, before modern medicine, I can agree with you that this was probably thought of as something supernatural. Believing their loved ones were possessed by some unseen, evil entity. But come now, in later times, it was all a combination of mental illness and hoaxes. I explained to you before, there are no influences by us on how people act, or what they do." Jeffrey returned his glasses to his face. "Now, I'm not saying that he doesn't end up with all the weak-minded ones. He certainly does.

The weak-minded make the worst decision-makers. But, it's still a roll of the dice with both of the ones in charge making their bets from the sidelines. It wouldn't be fair if either had the ability to turn the tables in one direction or another, now would it?"

"I suppose not."

"Ah, good then. I'm glad you understand. Now, next question."

"How long have I been here now?"

Jeffrey rolled his head in his aversion to the inquiry. "For goodness sake, Nick, would you please get off the subject of time? I can't make it any clearer. It simply doesn't exist, nor does it matter. Time is linear. It runs in a straight line that has no beginning and no end. You're overly obsessed with the concept of the wheel. A concept that has absolutely no meaning here."

"Just tell me."

"Fine, I'll indulge you." Jeffrey glanced around the room as if attempting to locate a clock on the dank walls or to find some sort of indication of just where this room was located in relation to the journey they'd traveled thus far. Or, possibly how far away the elevator may be from where they now sat. Jeffrey's upper lip disappeared into his lower as he frowned and threw out a guess, "I'd say about one thousand now."

Nick's eyes grew from behind his thick glasses. "One thousand years?! You're not being serious!"

Jeffrey looked over at Nick, "Well, of course, I'm being serious. Why, is that a problem?"

Nick pointed, "You're telling me that one thousand years have passed since we've been down here?!" He pointed towards the door, "That, that elevator is one thousand years away from here?!"

"Does it matter? Is it possible that you feel as if you haven't been here that long? Or perhaps you had somewhere to be in the third quarter of the millennium, and now you've missed your appointment? I've been telling you all along, Nick, the only thing that matters now is the theory of presentism, or possibly even externalism. Regardless, it doesn't make any difference at this point. Eternity is what it is. Right now is absolutely no different than it was when you stepped off that elevator. You have neither missed anything, nor have anything to look forward to. Everything from this point forward is only in the present for you. There is no past, nor any future for anyone down here."

"Oh, bullshit!" Nick's anger was brewing again, "Then how does the big dickhead know when to start someone's cycle again!? *Huh?!* Tell me!" Nick put his hands up to his chest as if defending himself from something and became sarcastic again, "Oh, I'm sorry, my bad. Was that not allowed either?! Did I call him by another proper name by mistake?!"

Jeffrey remained calm and self-centered, "Certainly not. He's been called worse, as I'm certain you have. And, to respond, each person's cycle isn't about time. Think of it more as a cyclical pattern. If you were to continually walk in a large circle, you would ultimately end up at the same point over and over again. Even if you turned around and began walking in the opposite direction, you're still going to end up in the same location, whether traveling backward or forward."

Jeffrey rested a finger on his forehead, and then pointed at Nick, "Think of it this way. A guinea pig runs as fast as it can on an exercise wheel. It never moves from its spot, however, it continually arrives in the same location on the wheel as it spins around him. The animal itself never moves, it's always in the present even though the wheel around it keeps going around and around. It doesn't matter how fast or slow the animal goes, he's always where he started even though the wheel keeps moving. It's the same thing here, my friend. You're nothing more than the guinea pig on a wheel that you cannot step off from, nor will you ever get anywhere."

"Terrific."

"Do you understand?"

"I don't really care." Nick meant his words. As in life, he was continuing to disregard the reality he now found himself within, and his host was taking note of the fact. Nick rolled his head and whined, "Just tell me, is this it? Is this all I'm going to see, a hallway that looks like the bowels of the Black Pearl?" Nick looked around the room, seeing nothing but emptiness, and a candle-lit hallway outside of the door. "Tell me, when do I get to see the Boss?!" Nick pointed at his chaperone, "Aren't I entitled? At least once?!" He motioned to his surroundings, "Where's his suite in this luxury hotel? Or doesn't he have time for special guests like me?!"

Jeffrey chortled and leaned back again, "What makes you think you're so special? Do you think you rank up there with the likes of Augusto Pinochet? Vladimir Lenin? Queen Mary?" He leaned in again, "Let me tell you something that you may not have figured out yet. You're nothing. In fact, you're less than nothing. Those others dictated countries for centuries. They tortured and killed thousands for personal gain, wealth, and notoriety. Or, to simply attempt to force their beliefs on others."

Jeffrey reached across the table and poked Nick in the shoulder, raising one eyebrow, "What did you ever do that could ever compare to the likes of them? Oh, sure, your crimes were disturbing, no doubt. They landed you here, didn't they? But, in the grand scheme of things you're just another pimple on the big, filthy ass of existence. Nothing more. Just a tiny speck of dirt under the feet of others far greater than you ever were."

Nick brushed the spot on his shirt where Jeff had laid a finger as if to move dust away and stared back without displaying any emotion.

"And, you truly think you have the right to see the Boss in person? Not to mention, what else did you expect to see down here? Did you think it was all going to resemble some massive, evil, big-top circus? That you were going to view vast wastelands as far as the eyes can see littered with people being tortured on crosses, or in the rat cages, or by garrote?"

Jeffrey was twirling his torso and motioning to the walls, "In case you hadn't figured it out yet, this place isn't meant to impress you, Nick. You aren't going to see any fiery pits, or sirens and demons dancing in the flames. In fact, I'm sorry to disappoint you, but you aren't going to see anything that will stimulate your senses at all. Except maybe your sense of fear. Nothing other than visions that will cause you pain and anguish, all meant to educate you about the ways of where you are. That's the name of the game, here, Sunshine."

"Stop calling me Sunshine."

Jeffrey leaned back again and adjusted his shoulders as if the comfortable cushions of the leather recliner were massaging his spine. He crossed his legs under the table and laid his left arm across his chest. His other elbow rested on his left hand. Near Jeffrey's mouth was his right hand, and between his fingers, Nick now saw a lit cigarette, whose filter disappeared into his host's mouth as he took a long drag. The lit end glowed from the heat of inhaling.

Nick's eyes widened and he blurted, "Where did you get a smoke?! I want one!"

Before Nick could lunge across the table and grab the burning nicotine stick, Jeffrey pulled it from his mouth and blew a long trail of smoke into the younger man's face. As the smoke mushroomed off his cheeks, Nick retreated back, coughing and gagging. The smoke hadn't smelled the sweet aroma of warm nicotine that he'd expected. Rather, it was an odor, and taste, of something far worse. Something not of Nick's earth. Something that made Nick nauseous, and he doubled over and vomited the acid and bile that upturned from his stomach onto the floor beside the table. He choked from the wretched taste, so vile that it caused him to slide from the bench to his knees, and he heaved violently on all fours until there was nothing left to bring up.

Jeffrey's expression reflected his arrogant amusement.

When he knew that Nick could hear again through his coughing and gagging, he spoke casually. "What's the matter, Nick? You appear to be a bit ill."

"Fuck you," Nick coughed, the last of the bile dripping from his chin as he spat onto the floor. He wiped his chin with the back of his hand while using the table to pull himself back up with his other arm. He spit once more on the floor before facing his host again.

Jeffrey cracked his signature smile and flicked the butt of the cigarette between his fingers. The cigarette took flight and the ash ricocheted as it bounced off the wall behind Nick, disappearing once landing on the floor. Jeffrey cocked his head and inquired endearingly, "Are you certain that you feel okay, Nick? You don't look well."

Nick slowly closed his eyes, and just as slowly opened them back up, somewhat defeated. He simply waited for Jeffrey to speak first.

"What did you expect, Nick? Did you really think he'd allow your senses to enjoy the rich, aromatic aroma of fine tobacco? Did you really believe that he'd allow you to enjoy the woody flavor, or bask in the soothing sensation of a drag off a cigarette just one more time? Because, if you did, you truly are a lost cause, and this journey has been for nothing."

Nick's shoulders raised and dropped, and another heavy sigh emitted his lips as he wiped the back of his hand on his trousers, "No days off, huh?"

Jeffrey perked up, "Very good, Nick. You're figuring it out. At least your sense of humor is still intact. That's something, now isn't it?"

Nick's dispirited but still sarcastic tone continued as he sat back on the bench, "So, let me see if I have this straight. I can't experience any pleasure. I won't eat and couldn't taste it anyway even if I could. Although, I'll feel terribly hungry. I won't drink, but I'll experience thirst. I won't smell anything sweet, only bad odors." Nick coughed, still able to taste the foul smoke and his own vomit. "I won't speak, only because there's nobody to talk to. There's no sex, not to mention no sex organs! Which means I won't piss, but I'll feel the need. I probably won't shit, but I'll bet any amount of money that I'll have cramps! I'll be awake for the rest of my existence and the senses that keep me awake and alert will be enhanced somehow. I can't go crazier than I already am. And, all I'll ever feel is pain and misery?! Is this all correct?! Did I leave anything out?!"

"Why Nick! You are finally beginning to understand!" Jeffrey was elated, "There's still a bit that you're missing, but you seem to have pinpointed the concept of where you are. I'm so pleased. Come now, it's time to continue our journey."

As the two stood, although he didn't want to return to the corridor, Nick was glad they were leaving this room behind.

Part 8

Nick's First Impression and the Theater on the Stairs

Jeffrey leaned forward and peered into the darkness, "I'm afraid we're going to need to go down from here."

The two stood at the top of a set of stairs that, instead of wood, appeared to have been constructed of weather-aged, cracked, and pitted granite slabs. Each piece of hardened earth being about a foot in depth and equal in width to that of the corridor. The walls remained the same aging timbers and rough, hand-hewn wooden rafters above with no ceiling in sight. Instead of the chandeliers, there were single candelabras along the walls every eight steps. The stairway was steep and as Nick leaned to look down, he could see no bottom in the darkness below.

"At least it's down and not up," Jeffrey noted.

"Where do they go?"

"Nowhere, to coin a metaphor. They go where all of these passageways go. And, somewhere down there is your space."

"That's encouraging."

"Hold on to that sense of humor, Nick. As we draw

nearer, you're going to need it."

"How far down do they go?"

"Oh, quite a distance, I'm afraid. However, it really doesn't matter, now does it? But, don't worry, there are things to be seen along the way."

As the two began to descend, Nick believed he could make out the familiar sounds of crying and moaning coming from below. Far, far below, he thought as he strained to listen. It also became apparent that every twenty or so steps there appeared a wider granite landing, about six feet long and Nick thought possibly it wasn't a straight drop, that somehow the stairwell was taking a gradual turn similar to a spiral staircase. Only, that it seemed to turn in both directions at intervals. Nick felt that at some point along the descent, a door would appear on either side of one of the landings when Jeffrey felt it appropriate to create one.

As it would turn out, Nick would be correct. After what felt like an eternity, so to speak, the two stopped on one of the landings where a door to either side had now revealed themselves. Nick glanced back up the stairs, and then below, with a slight feeling of basophobia washing over him as he still couldn't see any end in sight below him, nor anything above either.

He was startled when the new voice spoke out.

"Can you help me?" The voice was trembling and cracked, like a very old man's voice. His tone was deep in bass as if he was speaking through amplified speakers. Nick looked up to see a face at the tiny window to the door on his right. The opening on this door being just a touch larger, maybe eight inches square, and just a bit lower than the others by an inch or so. Nick's eyes widened and then he squinted in the low light in an effort to make out the man's features. All he could see was half of the man's face. One eye, a nose, and a wrinkled brow looking down at him. The remainder in the shadows and out of his view. The man's skin resembled aged leather and he had gray facial hair and equally graying head hair stringing down over what could be seen of his face.

Nick turned to look up at Jeff, "Who's that?"

Jeffrey's eyebrows lifted up, "*Hmmm*. Let's see. I'm not exactly certain. Just wait, though, it'll come to me. Hold on."

"It hurts so terribly. Please, help me." Nick turned back to look up at the old man. His own anger and frustration turned to a bit of compassion for the voice speaking down to him from the other side of the door.

"I'm still thinking." Jeffrey glanced up and down. "It's difficult to say which area we're in. Oh, well. Regardless, he shouldn't be talking to you. Another rule, no speaking."

Nick's demeanor turned sour again as he turned back to his host. "No talking? You can't be serious. You can't talk down here either? Not even to yourself?"

"Certainly not. We've discussed this, Nick. That would be another form of stimulation that simply isn't allowed. Not even to yourself." Jeff pointed to the window. "I'm afraid he'll be punished severely for interrupting our journey and speaking out like that. We didn't ask him to."

Nick motioned to the door with both arms, "He isn't interrupting anything! He just wants someone to talk to! Cut the poor guy a break, why don't you?!"

"I'm sorry, it simply isn't allowed. Anyway, it's his rules, not mine. There's simply no talking allowed. Only crying and screaming out in pain, two completely uncontrollable actions of the human brain. A spontaneous reaction, if you will. Talking isn't spontaneous, that's a planned action. The motor cortex of the frontal lobe sending deliberate signals to the muscles of the mouth, throat, and tongue to form words..."

"I know what talking is!"

"There's no more deliberate actions for you to take down here, Nick. Everything is laid out for you in advance. All you need to do is sit, and wait. And, keep your mouth shut. All you have here is the power of thought, no other. Plus, you must even learn to control that." Jeffrey thought for a moment, "Although, I suppose you could consider the power of thought to be a form of talking to yourself, now couldn't you? Well, there you go, then. You can think, just not out loud, and hope he doesn't hear you." Jeffrey smiled.

"I can't even think to myself without getting into trouble?! *That's bullshit!*"

"Please. The pain is too much. Help me." The man's tone was low, desperate, and pleading.

Nick turned back to the door. His own voice was sincere, "I can't help you. I'm sorry. I wish I could."

This was the first time that the young man had shown any compassion since arriving, something not going unnoticed by his host. "Why would you want to help him?" Jeffrey's voice hinted at both arrogance and sarcasm.

Nick's head spun around. "Can't you see this guy's in pain?"

"Of course he is. What else is there for him now? Have you forgotten where you are? You don't think that you won't be experiencing the exact same thing very soon, now do you? You don't think that you won't be staring out of your own little window to the next one that walks by? And, wanting to beg them for help just as he is? You can't help him. You can't even help yourself." Jeffrey pointed to the window again. "Take note, Nick. Don't do what he's doing. Don't make the same mistakes he's making."

Nick's head turned back and he saw tears streaming down that part of the old man's face that he could make out.

"Please. It will happen again soon. I know it will. The pain. I can't take it anymore. Have mercy. Make it stop."

"What happens to you?" Nick spoke softly.

"Please, Nick. That's quite inappropriate. You aren't helping him at all. You're just making it worse. Why do you seek to harm this man?"

"I want to know!" Even though Nick was staring straight at the old man, his words were directed at Jeffrey.

"He can't tell you. He's not allowed."

"Who is he?!"

"He's nobody, Nick."

"Please. The pain. Oh…*God!*" The old man's voice raised, and the eye that Nick could make out began to grow wider as the veins on his wrinkled forehead threatened to burst.

Nick pleaded, "No! Don't say that! *You can't say that!*"

"I don't understand why you'd want to hurt this man." Jeffrey's tone remained calm and consistent from behind, "I'm afraid you haven't helped him a bit. We should go before it gets any worse. He did nothing to you, Nick. Why do you feel the need to cause him more harm than he already receives?"

Nick's head had turned again as he addressed his host with anger, "Worse?! What do you mean?! I'm not the one hurting him! I'm not doing anything to him!"

"You've caused this poor man to break the rules. In fact, you've encouraged it." Jeff smiled through his words and boasted, "Although the Boss is certainly impressed with you for doing so. I'm afraid this man's suffering is going to be so much more intense now due to his weak-mindedness. All because of you, Nicholas."

"I didn't do anything!" Nick turned back again to see the old man's face trembling. He lowered his voice again, "What's happening to him?"

Jeffrey peered through the door's opening over Nick's head and responded casually, "I'm afraid that for his ignorance and stupidity, he must begin his next cycle earlier than usual. And, with his pain intensified to a much greater extent than before. We really should go now before you make it any worse for him. He's about to experience things that he wasn't prepared for. Pity, really. Before you came along his suffering was intense enough, but he did have his actions somewhat under control. He really didn't deserve this. You're a bad influence, Nick."

Nick watched as the old man's trembling continued to worsen, and the eye that begged for mercy began to trickle blood which streamed down over the man's deeply wrinkled and recessed face. Nick was helpless to act, nor would he have known what to do even if he were to be allowed entry into the man's room. Nick stared intently, powerless and with his mouth hanging open. The old man's bulging eye looked down at Nick, whose own eyes looked behind the man's head when he saw a shadow approaching. Nick knew without being told that a demon in the form of an executioner had appeared behind the poor soul.

The destitute old man let out one more high-pitched scream as the iron Warhammer was swung. Nick's eyes grew wider as he watched the man's head violently explode, or at least the part of his head that Nick had the ability to see. Blood and brain matter drenched the door and flew from the window opening. The flesh struck Nick in his face as it ricocheted off the thick wood of the window frame and splashed down. The warm blood and pieces stuck to Nick's lenses, covered his face, and flew into his open mouth. It also ejected straight outward and struck Jeffrey in his head, oozing down his face and staining the front of his shirt.

Nick only momentarily continued to stare in shock through his crimson-red lenses, not immediately fully comprehending what had occurred as he began to hear the deafening screams of the old man increase in pitch. He knew, though, that even without part of his head, the old man was fully aware of every bit of pain he was experiencing, only now to be intensified by simply speaking out. Nick covered both of his ears, gagged, and coughed as he bent forward and spit the old man's warm flesh back out.

Jeffrey simply removed his own glasses and began to wipe them on his blood-stained shirt, seemingly unimpressed and unaffected by what was occurring.

Another swing of the massive hammer and the screaming suddenly ceased. Jeffrey began to pick brain matter from his well-combed hair and dropped the pieces to the granite below. "Well now, we have you to thank for that, now haven't we?"

Nick hadn't heard the words through his own retching as he was doubled over and coughing up the old man's life fluid, plus pieces of skull bone, and throwing up his own stomach contents once again.

"That's unfortunate." Jeff continued in monotone, "Still though, not surprising. You sort of deserve that." Jeffrey picked another chunk of matter from his hair, looked at it, and flicked it to the stone steps below his feet.

Nick, now down on one knee, looked up as he wiped the phlegm from his chin, along with blood that now stained his face, and bits of the old man's frontal lobe. He glanced as black smoke began to billow from the door's window and plume in the empty air above the two. The odor in the corridor now changed from one of old, moldy wet wood and candle wax to one of flesh cooking.

"He's burning to death, isn't he?" Nick inquired as he continued to cough while attempting to stand himself back up.

"I wouldn't say to death. But, yes, that's one thing that's occurring. Along with the zombies. The undead so enjoy warm, fresh meat. Although, I wouldn't say burning exactly, more like simmering, or possibly smoldering. Sort of like bread in a toaster. Or perhaps condiments on a fryolator. A slow cook really."

"You're sick." Nick was fully back to his feet, still coughing and picking chunks from his own hair. "I thought everyone was dead down here."

"I said undead. Try to pay attention."

With the screaming now ceased, Nick surmised that the old man's vocal cords were gone, or possibly his entire head. He also realized that it didn't matter and that the old man's pain was continuing without the ability to cry out as thick, dark smoke continued to pour from the window. The flickering of flames from behind the door reflected through the frame and other deep crevices in the woodwork.

Jeffrey looked Nick up and down, and then at himself. "Good job, by the way."

Nick cleaned his own glasses with his hands and looked his host over as he wiped the last of the blood and puke from his chin. With his sarcasm returning and his retching now completed, he replied in his signature, snarky tone after spitting to the floor, "I'm sure the stains will come out."

Nick turned back to the door and looked it up and down as he listened to the flames from within burn and detected the crackling sounds of flesh and bone, along with the smell of same. The door was now stained a dark red just below the window, with chunks of flesh among the drippings. Nick thought he heard gurgling and the sound of chewing. He winced, disgusted by the odor and audibles, and felt that he may throw up again.

Jeffrey continued to wipe from his shirt what he believed to be hypothalamus, and what appeared to be pituitary gland, as he'd know from experience. "I don't think I'll introduce you to the resident across the way. You seem to have an issue with first impressions. We should just keep moving."

Nick looked past Jeffrey to see another doorway on the opposite side of the landing. It was secured the same as all the others with heavy, rusting chains through the door's wooden handle to a large, iron O-ring mounted to the frame, and a rusted padlock connecting the chains. Nick glanced to the window and saw the shadow of someone standing back from the door reflecting in the low light of the room.

Nick also felt that he too didn't really need to meet the occupant right at that moment, and he started back down the stairs, following his host.

◆ ◆ ◆

Nick saw what he thought to be a light in the darkness below him that didn't appear to be coming from the candles as the two continued down the solid rock stairwell. He squinted to see better, the light was emitting maybe four or five landings below. The yellowish-white glowing became brighter as the two descended further. When they stepped on the landing just above, Nick thought he could hear music coming from the direction of the light. Nick also took notice in the better light that Jeffrey's clothing was clean again, and there were no indications of the incident that occurred just above them only a short time earlier. Or rather, what Nick believed to be only a few minutes gone by. Nick checked his own clothing and discovered the same; he was once again clean and free of someone else's blood and flesh. He removed his glasses to make certain. He inspected them, they were also clean.

The two continued down, and what revealed itself to either side of the landing were two sets of large double doors opposite of each other. Both sets were open and the yellowish glow was illuminating from each doorway. The sounds from inside were loud and distinct as the two men stood between the doors.

"My apartment?"

"Not quite." Jeffrey was unamused with the comment. He guided his apprentice through the doors to one side. Nick stepped through and discovered what appeared to be a massive theater. It looked to Nick as if the room intersected the stairwell to the set of doors on the opposite side, although in reality, it couldn't as the granite stairwell continued down when Nick stuck his head back outside to look.

Jeffrey tugged his apprentice back into the room. The young man looked around the impressive space, which again appeared that any possible ceiling had been replaced with night sky the same as the library, and another brighter moon, not the same as the one before. This time it appeared to be in the Waning Crescent phase. It reflected light off the billions of stars surrounding it.

Nick looked down to see, far away, a large carousel in the center of the theater. From what he could make out it looked very old. Antique, with the white and black horses each displaying terrible, ugly expressions. They also didn't appear as calm, trotting horses. They were all in a bucking stance as if involved in a battle with their invisible riders attacking each other with swords and shields. The top of the carousel had a tall, pointed red and white tapestry and the music blaring to the rotation of the bobbing horses sounded as if were coming from a large, old circus pipe organ. Although boisterous, it also sounded many miles away to Nick, and its eerie music echoed off the night sky.

To either side of the carousel were not rows of seats, but rather dozens of connecting buildings. Structures that each resembled the front of castles and fanciful houses. Each painted brilliant colors, some with fairy-tale, pointed rooftops, and others displaying bell towers. They were tall structures, at least two stories high and some were three. All the upper stories had balconies and running down the middle was a continuous, winding brick catwalk mounted to the exterior. The catwalk wasn't straight, but rather wavy, as if many years had caused the buildings to lose their leveling from the uneven earth they were built upon. The actual coloration of the buildings was hard to make out due to the night's darkness above and the moonlight was causing a glow to each building it shined down upon. On the ground surrounding the carousel and along the front of the buildings were large cauldrons containing fires that also reflected off the structures, again making the colors appear to change in the flickering flames. Nick squinted through his lenses and felt as if he saw the reflection of demons in the flames. He thought that possibly it was just the place itself affecting his imagination. He then looked to the carousel and again found it had no riders, nor were there any patrons standing at any of the balconies, nor on the catwalks either.

The stage sat on the far end of the theater. It was enormous. A large set of steps, maybe twenty feet high, led to a polished stone landing. The stage itself was possibly forty feet wide and the same deep. Behind it was a large tapestry, dark maroon. It too stood many feet and seemed to float in the air at its highest point. To each side of the stage were several large, granite pillars. At the top of each were mounted cauldrons of fire that illuminated the floor below, and reflected in the darkness of night above. Between the two sets of buildings, surrounding the carousel and extending to the colossal stage appeared to be a walkway made of old cobblestone. Again, vacant of life, or life-after-death.

Everything that Nick was viewing, the buildings, carousel, and stage, were below him. Another winding set of stairs descending from both entrances circled down to the cobblestone below. The number of stairs had to be in the hundreds, if not more, Nick thought. And the stairwell itself was covered in maroon and ebony-designed carpeting. At the top of the stairs where the two stood there was a railing, as if they were standing on a high balcony. Although it was only one single room it felt like a small village to Nick with the buildings, walkways, and sky above. And, although it felt as such, Nick continued to experience the overwhelming sensation of claustrophobia.

"What is this place?"

"Isn't it obvious, Nick? It's his theater. A place which brings him much joy and amusement, although to no other."

Nick was in awe as his eyes and mind attempted to take it all in. "What happens in here?"

Jeffrey spoke proudly, standing straight and looking out, "Well, Nick. I think you'll like this. You see, he isn't without…well, let's not use the term *mercy*. Let's just say he's open to allowing you a little game of chance. But, only if you're up for it. Plus, he so loves the theater." Jeffrey folded his arms across his chest and looked out over the spectacle before them. "That is if the play is indeed a good one. You see, Nick, when he's feeling like indulging, he hand picks a chosen few. Now, you have the right to participate, or you may choose not to. It's completely up to you. If you choose to be a character, of which he chooses the part in which you'll play, you will be required to act in his production in return for the chance to skip one entire cycle."

Jeff turned to Nick and raised a finger. "However, the chance you take is that your cycle was, in fact, scheduled to begin during the performance. If not, you still have to endure it as soon as the play concludes. Otherwise, you are free of the normal punishment you would have received during that one performance."

Leaning against the rail and looking down, "Okay, what's the catch? Are you in trouble if you forget a line or something?" Nick reared his hand back when the splinter entered his left pointer finger. He angrily shook his hand in pain and disgust.

"Ah, the catch. Yes, there always must be a catch. I certainly agree. Well, the catch is, Nick, that the part you play in his production comes with its own…well, let's say discomfort." Jeffrey motioned with both arms to the room and boasted, "You see, my dear Nicholas, the production you are agreeing to take part in is Shakespeare's first tragedy, Titus Andronicus. A particularly violent little play, I must admit. Or, rather a modified version of it." Jeffrey chuckled, "You can't begrudge him a bit of alteration to the script, now can you? After all, it is for his sole enjoyment." Jeffrey pointed a finger to the air, "You see, he adjusts the violence just a bit to enhance it to his liking."

Nick continued to soak in the room, listening to what his host was telling him and sucking on his finger.

Jeffrey displayed an evil grin and leaned down to Nick. "Now, if you know anything about the play, you'll know that Lavinia's part has her tongue and hands cut off. The parts of Martius and Quintus have their heads severed, and Tamora is eaten by wild beasts while the part of Aaron is hanged. All quite entertaining. So, he adds to it just a bit more. Adding a disembowelment or two here, and a flaying there. Just to enhance the atmosphere, mind you. And, voila, you have a production! A very live performance!" Jeffrey's tone turned to one of reasoning, "The little additions are nothing, really. And, all of it is certainly far less agonizing than anyone's normal cycle, so it's really a win-win for everyone. That is, of course, unless it wasn't scheduled correctly and the player must endure all that, plus their normal punishment. That would certainly be a bummer, now wouldn't it? Ah, well, it happens. That's the chance they take, Nick."

The young man turned slowly and stared at his host, a most unimpressive, boorish stare. Somewhat amazed by what he was hearing.

Jeffrey stood looking out, raised a hand, and continued his boasting, "Of course, the players are required to continue acting even after enduring what their parts require of them in the form of punishment and pain, per the script. A bit difficult for those who've been disemboweled, I must say. Having to carry around that extra bit of entrails dangling from their bodies isn't easy. It affects their acting terribly. Not that they were any good at acting, to begin with."

Jeffrey turned and winked at his pupil, "You know, the nervousness of memorizing lines, the violent trembling of knowing what their character will endure. Those sorts of trivial things. Of course, for the two that lose their heads, their parts are basically over at that point. Regardless, they're required to remain on stage throughout the duration of the play. You know, be good sports and all until the final curtain call. I suppose you could say they become spectators at that point for the duration, now couldn't you? So, there you go. Not only do they get to act in the play, but they also get to see how it ends." Jeffrey turned away from Nick and laughed out loud at his own words, his voice echoing out over the emptiness of the theater.

"You're sick."

Jeffrey snapped back, "Of course, I am. Just like you!" He cackled insanely again. And with the raise of an eyebrow, "That's why we're here!"

Jeffrey returned to his usual demeanor, "Think of it as a snuff film, Nick. However, nobody really dies in the end, now do they? They're already dead to begin with, just like you and I." Jeffrey's pompous tone never waned, "So, you see, Nick, he does allow a bit of recreation and fun. You just might get the chance to act in his play and, if you're lucky, your pain cycle for once will be replaced with something entirely different. The lesser of the two evils, you could say."

"Okay, Einstein! What if he's just screwing with them?!" Nick removed his finger from his mouth and pointed out towards the stage, "Doesn't he get to decide when your cycle arrives? What if you choose to act in his little play, and he still bends you over the table afterward?! What then brainiac?!"

With a raise of both eyebrows above the rims of his glasses and a hand to his own chin, his host responded, *"Hmmm.* I never thought of that. That's good thinking, Nick. And here all the while I thought your intelligence was rather lacking the power of logical thought and deliberation."

Nick shook his head slowly, cleverly choosing to not indulge his host and risk further insult.

"A chance you'll have to take, I suppose, if you're lucky enough to be chosen. Something to ponder if provided with the opportunity. Good one, Nick." Jeffrey began to turn and then stopped himself, "But then again, Nick, don't forget, what about the wheel we spoke of? What if everyone's cycle is really a predestined event occurring regularly, and the play itself occurs spontaneously somewhere along that spectrum? Then, it really is a game of chance, now isn't it?"

Nick had a thought, "Wait a minute!" Nick shook his head at the reference to time and then continued. "A play taking place when a cycle was either due to happen or not! That would be a reference to time, wouldn't it?!"

An evil grin formed on Jeffrey's face, "My, my, Nick. An actual thought from a conscious, cognitive process. An actual mental event of perception. I'm impressed."

"Whatever! Am I right?!"

"Who's to say, Nick? Remember, time doesn't matter

here."

Defeated once again, "This place is too confusing."

"Not really, Nick. Actually, it's all quite simple." Jeffrey looked at his wrist again, where there was still no watch to be found. "We should go. Another production is about to begin and he certainly can't allow you the pleasure of being a spectator, now can he? We can't allow you to have a bite of that apple, now can we? I'm certain you'd enjoy that far too much. Come along now."

◆ ◆ ◆

"Ah, here we are." The two stepped down into a corridor at the bottom of the stone landing. The new, old, dark passageway went both left and right. Its construction and lighting were identical to the corridors at the top of the granite stairwell.

Jeffrey peered in both directions, pointing to his right, "Now, that's an interesting pathway down there." He looked to his friend, "That's where all the cult leaders are kept. There are so many types, too. The doomsayers, the political ones. The terrorists, polygamists, and racist ones. So many. Nasty business too, if you ask me. Again, using religion as a means of wealth, power, greed, and sex. Just terrible. A very overpopulated area, down that way."

Nick adjusted his glasses to the bridge of his nose and he blinked his eyes from behind the thick lenses, looking in the direction his host had motioned. "You mean all those just like the guy who made his followers drink the Kool-Aid and stuff?"

"Yes, and many more. And yes, certainly, the leader of the People's Temple, as you so colorfully described. He's down there. Along with all the others that used their influence for things other than true religious reasons. It's ironic, don't you think? People like that promising reward and salvation to their followers, only to take advantage of them in ways you wouldn't expect them to. All the while attempting to force some ridiculous religious beliefs that they themselves don't even buy into. Or, worse, are fanatical about." Jeffrey turned to his student, "Not to mention the power they hold over other entities, like government, or even law enforcement. It's the greed that makes me laugh. As if any religion requires their leaders to be wealthy, live in castles, and drive expensive cars. The big guy doesn't like these types at all."

"Okay, so, what's the Kool-Aid guy get?"

Jeffrey peered down the corridor as if he could see the person they were referencing directly in his line of sight. "Ah, yes. Well, it's quite unique. And, quite ironic when you think about it." He turned back to Nick, "His torture was perfected in the 17th century, which is where, as I mentioned earlier in our walk, so many religious zealots also attempted to force their beliefs on others. You see, my dear Nicholas, he receives a form of impalement commonly referred to as longitudinal. Do you know what this is, Nick?"

"The longi..?"

Jeffrey waived his hand and cut the young man off, rather arrogantly, "No, I thought not. Well, Nick, allow me to elaborate. He's laid face down with his arms bound behind him. The executioners then drive a dry, pointed stake into his anus and up through his torso, ending up in his throat. It exits through his mouth, which certainly makes it impossible for him to scream, let alone breathe very well. It's a very long stake, I might add too, not to mention about three inches in diameter."

Jeffrey hesitated and chuckled before continuing, "He's then raised up as the butt of the stake is shoved into the ground, and he slowly slides down the length of it. In terms of longevity of the situation, because we don't want to mention that time thing again you know. Well, let's just say his predicament from start to finish isn't exactly instantaneous. In fact, quite the contrary. You see, the stake is barbed from end to end, and the barbs are not pointing in the direction that one would prefer. It takes quite a while to complete the process. Obviously, that's not all that he endures, but you get the picture, don't you Nick?"

"Yeah. Sounds like good times."

"If you say so, Nick."

Nicholas stretched his neck out to see down the dark passageway as he continued, "What about that fruit loop from Waco, Texas?" Turning back to his host, "Or those idiots that thought the Hale-Bopp comet was coming to take them into outer space?"

"Well, to answer your first inquiry, yes, he's here. As far as the latter, you can't simply punish people for believing in ridiculous things like that, now can you? However, you can punish the ones that drove that belief into their feeble minds and caused them to do what they did, just like the Kool-Aid man."

Nick felt he had another epiphany, and he pointed, "Wait, but what about all those followers? They all committed suicide, didn't they? Isn't that a mortal sin?"

"Oh, come now, Nick," Jeffrey rolled his eyes, along with his head just slightly, "Now you're talking about references to religious beliefs again. We've discussed this. You can't blame the feeble-minded for what they do, or what they're driven to do by others. You can only blame the source that plants the ideas that they eventually act upon. What you're talking about is no different than punishing people for committing acts in violation of one of the seven capital vices. Or, even sending those that do so to purgatory. My goodness, Nick, I've mentioned before, if that were the case the top floor would be entirely empty. A castle without servants. A king without a kingdom to rule over."

"But, they could be forgiven, right?"

Jeffrey pointed, "And, so they are, Nick. We simply can't be so nitpicky. The human race is bad enough without overloading the middle plain, or this place, with all those who violate one of Aristotle's Nicomanchean Ethics. We simply don't have the room."

Both Nick and Jeffrey's attention turned to the corridor to the right again, as they heard an intense shrieking coming from nearby, or what was believed to be closer to where they were standing rather than in a distance.

"Who was that?!" Another blood-curdling scream traveled the passageway following Nick's inquiry. The young man felt a tingling in his spine as the wailing echoed, shooting through his body as it raced through the corridor.

Jeffrey responded nonchalantly as he peered in the direction of the screaming, "Ah, that would be the self-proclaimed leader of Scientology." His head returned to face his young apprentice, "The one from your time, to be specific. Not the one before him that created the organization. He just wrote books. He isn't here, yet." Jeffrey glanced back to the location of the continuous, and obvious response to someone's agonizing pain. "You know, the one that made his wife disappear and punished his followers on a whim. That's him."

Another blood-curdling cry of pain echoed off the dark walls and Nick's eyes grew as the piloerection formed on his forearms and neck. "What's happening to him?"

Jeffrey looked down, closed his eyes, and slowly shook his head. "You don't really want to know. Unfortunately for him, he's one of the master's favorites. The Boss just loves it when someone twists the big man's beliefs for their own personal gain." Jeffrey opened his eyes back and directed himself towards the continuous shrieking. "And his punishment certainly reflects that fact." He turned back to his apprentice, "Just be glad that's not you."

Nick tried to ignore the agonizing sounds, turning away. "Fine. So, what's in the other direction?"

Jeffrey perked up and turned his attention to the other end of the corridor. "Ah, yes. Well, Nick, that would be your wing. You know, all the pathetic active shooters. The school shooters, the disgruntled ones that kill their fellow employees, the random building snipers. All the ones that commit random acts of violence against society for reasons of anger, fame, or simply hatred."

Nick glared down the corridor, a hint of concern on his face that didn't go unnoticed by his host. Nick realized for a moment that he may be nearing the end of their journey together. As he gazed down the passageway, he immediately took note that he could now see rows and rows of doorways to either side and as far as he could see until darkness shrouded whatever was beyond his sight.

"My, my, Nick. What's the matter? You look a bit concerned."

"Nothing!" Nick forced his poor attitude to return. "How come I can see so many doorways now?"

"Because, Nick, you have a lot of people to meet down there. Why not introduce you around to your neighbors? Isn't that what you wanted, Nick? For people to know who you were? Wasn't that the point?"

Nick turned to look up at Jeffrey, annoyed by his host's arrogant grin. "Why would I want to meet any of them?!" Nick flinched when the screaming ceased at the moment that a loud bone-crushing noise echoed from the direction of the cult leader who'd been crying out.

Jeffrey ignored the grotesque sounds. "Well, wasn't it your goal to be just like them? Don't you want to blend in with all of those like you? Let's see, at last count, I believe we were well into the thousands of pathetic active shooters just like you." Jeffrey cocked his head, "Possibly you felt that you would stand out among them? That you were somehow special? That maybe you weren't just the same as any other faceless fool that walked into a school and randomly killed children?"

"Screw you."

"Ah, yes. That seems to be a typical response from you, Nick, now doesn't it?" Jeffrey perked up, "Anyway. Name somebody, anybody from that section. I'm certain that you can, can't you? Didn't they all become famous, as they thought they would by committing a one-time random act of violence? Just the same as you felt that you would? Name one, Nick. Just one, and I'll introduce you."

Nick turned and glared at Jeffrey. "You think you're real funny, don't you? You think I can't name one? Okay, fine! Columbine!"

Jeffrey glared straight back, "I didn't say name the school, or the location, Nicholas. I said to name the shooter. One name, Nick. One simple, full name. You can't, can you?" Jeffrey cocked his head upwards, "Oh, you can name serial killers, cult leaders, or maybe even famous wife murderers. They're easy." He glared and pointed, "But, you can't name one person that did the same thing that you did, all believing that they'd be famous for doing it. Not one, can you? And, do you know why? Because, my dear Nicholas, you're all nothing. I've been telling you this all along."

Jeffrey pointed down the corridor while his eyes were still locked on Nick's, his tone demeaning, "Not one of them became anything. And, I'll tell you something else! None of them were anything, to begin with! Just pathetic excuses for human beings. Simply the weak ones that couldn't take what life was dishing out." He pointed and bent towards his pupil, speaking softly, "They're the quitters, Nick. Just like you. The ones that felt the only way to make a mark in their life was to take another's. And, ultimately, not only did society throw them away, well guess what? So does the big man upstairs. You see, Nick, he only wants the strong. The winners. Not the likes of you."

Nick's glaring resulted in what appeared to Jeffrey to be a tear, which the young man was fighting back terribly. Jeffrey stood and perked back up, smiled, and remarked jovially, "Well, it doesn't matter now. Does it, Nick? Just like you, they've all fallen into obscurity. All the little bitches just sitting in their tiny, little rooms, waiting for their pain to arrive again. All wishing now that they'd made better choices in life. Well, now, we should go meet a few. Come along."

When Jeffrey turned away to lead Nick down the passageway, the tear he'd been fighting streamed down his face. Nick quickly wiped it away.

◆ ◆ ◆

After passing by several of the doorways, Jeffrey suddenly stopped. "Ah, now, here we have someone you might be interested in. One of the first known school shooters to be documented properly." Jeffrey, with an arm back around Nick's shoulders, turned to the young man. "She was bored, Nick. That's all. And, really, she put no effort into her crime. She didn't even bother to leave her own home to commit them. She pointed her gun straight out of her bedroom window and there, across the street, was the elementary school." Jeffrey peered through the door's window, which once again was tiny and only at his eye level. "One moment of stupidity to relieve the doldrums. That's all it took, Nick. And, now she's here, sitting, and waiting."

"Just because she was bored?"

Still peering inside the room, "Let's just say that she didn't like Mondays." He looked at Nick and smiled, "She also has a nasty aversion to scaphism. Come along now."

"Wait! What is scaphism?"

Jeffrey sighed, "Well, to put it lightly, she's covered in milk and honey and placed between two small boats, tied down to one and the other placed on top. All in a very hot environment, I might add. The boats aren't exactly air tight either, allowing many nasty creatures to sneak in. You know, large insects, rats, other small vermin, things like that. Over…well, time." Jeffrey chuckled, "Sorry."

Nick flashed a dirty smirk.

"Anyway, she's eaten rather slowly. Oh, and the creatures like to use her…well, orifices. Small creatures like to tunnel and burrow, so it's not entirely a feasting from the outside in. It's more of the inside-out. The boats don't exactly muffle her screaming, either. Because, you know, she's quite aware during the ordeal and very vocal."

Nick felt the now-familiar feeling in his stomach again as

Jeffrey prompted the two away from the door. Nick's head snapped around when he heard terrible screaming from ahead of them.

Jeffrey remained calm, "Ah, here we go. Right up here to the left. I believe that was Dylan."

"Who?" Another high-pitched shrieking followed the inquiry. It came from the next doorway to their left along the dank corridor.

"Oh, come now, Nicholas. I thought you were familiar with the occurrence in Colorado. You mentioned it yourself, now didn't you?" The two stopped in front of the doorway where Nick quickly realized the noises were bellowing from. "Anyway, here we have one-half of the duo."

"Who is it?"

Jeffrey's tone was one of defeat, "You disappoint me, Nick. I thought at least you'd be familiar with this one…" His words were cut off by another scream that sent chills through Nick's entire body. Even Jeffrey winced as he peered through the window opening. "Nasty, nasty punishment." He looked down at Nick and frowned, "I'm glad that's not me in there."

"Pleeeease! S-s-s-top! Aaaahhhheeeee! Unnnggghhhh!"

Nick strained, "What?! *What is that?!*" This time, rather than his question being presented as inquisitive amusement, or sarcasm, it was received with concern and apprehension as more ear-piercing screams emitted from the room.

"Help Me-e-e-e! Aaahhhhhhunghhh!"

"What's happening in there?!"

"Do you really want to know?" Jeffrey's tone was eerily calm, and his smile evil as he folded his arms and leaned against the doorframe.

"Yes! *Please!*" Nick was pleading. Almost begging for knowledge of what was happening to the person inside this room. In turn, his mind was unconsciously comparing the poor soul's punishment to what he, himself, might endure soon.

Jeffrey's expression was a combination of amusement

and befuddlement as he looked at his pupil, "You still seem terribly distracted by the punishments of others, Nick. That concerns me. You really should be more worried about yourself."

"Just let me see! I need to know!" The veins in Nick's neck were straining terribly and his head bobbing in his attempts to see through the tiny window or possibly through a crack in the door. He was determined to know what the person on the opposite side was experiencing. The terrible, incoherent cries of pain were calling out to Nick. He needed to get at least a glimpse of what just might be his own torture that would, no doubt, be arriving sooner than he would ever be prepared for.

A heavy sigh along with his grin, "Alright. If you must." Jeffrey stood back up, raised a hand to the chains on the door, and they fell to the floor. Nick looked up with astonishment and discovered that Jeffrey's evil smile bothered him.

"Go ahead, Nick. Open it and see."

Nick's hand hesitated, only for a moment, and then he reached for the door's massive, wooden handle as another agonizing cry of pain echoed. Before he could reach the handle, Jeffrey reared back and kicked the door open, startling his young apprentice. The door crashed into the interior wall to reveal not a small room, but what appeared to be a massive chamber of torture, quite possibly in the bottom of some ancient castle. Nick's eyes saw what appeared to be decaying, moldy stone walls whose purpose may have been to muffle the screams of anguish only just a bit, and a dirt floor replaced the corridor's wooden one. In the center of the room was a large, wooden structure resembling an oversized ladder. One end was planted to the floor with the other raised towards the rounded stone ceiling, all mounted on logs. On either end were large rollers with ropes extending to the center where the victim lay, stretched out on his back.

The man being tortured appeared young, maybe in his

mid-to-late teens. He didn't appear athletic, but rather normal in size. He looked like any other boy next door. In fact, quite the same as Nick. He was naked and again, appeared fully intact as far as extremities, at least for the time being. The ropes were tied to his wrists, extending to the roller above, and on his ankles to the roller below. The bindings were taught, stretching the young man out. Standing on the floor in control of the rollers was a demon, the executioner. He was dressed in period clothing with thick, canvas rags that formed a smock with a hood over his faceless head and ropes tied around his waist. The cloth he wore was dirty and frayed. His massive, hairy arms and legs extended out of the torn clothing. He was operating the mechanism, stretching the man out further in increments with each turn of the rollers.

However, this wasn't what appeared to be causing the poor soul the worst of his pain. Also standing on a wooden platform nearer the center of the rack was a second henchman, identical to the first. This creature had his hands on a metal handle with a large screw extending from it, and a large wingnut at the top of the screw. The screw penetrated the prisoner's stomach, which appeared distended. Blood was flowing over his lower torso from the wound, dripping from his genitals and staining the wooden contraption and the gravel floor below as it rained down. The henchman was turning the screw at the wing, which appeared to be causing the piercing screaming far more than the stretching was.

Nick's voice remained low in tone, "What are they doing to him? Where is he?"

Jeffery stood just inside the doorway with Nick, his arm back around the young man's shoulder. "He's in his place of pain. The place he goes during every cycle. They're stretching him on a rack, Nick. A device that can be dated back to the period of antiquity and lasting many thousands of years. You see, Nick, the one on the floor is stretching every fiber of that man's muscles which will cause his joints to dislocate, and eventually break."

"What's that thing in his stomach?"

Jeffrey bent to Nick's level and pointed, "Ah, now that would be something called a Pearl of Anguish. A device of the early modern period created sometime in the 1600s. You see, Nick, they cut a hole just below his sternum near the base of his ribcage and then pack it with clay to avoid as much bleeding as possible. They then insert the device. The part of it that you can't see is pear-shaped, made up of four long, spoon-like pieces of metal with very sharp edges. As the screw on the top of the handle is turned, the spoons expand out from the center, creating a void and placing pressure on all of the organs surrounding it. It's quite painful, as you can see. Lucky for him, though, they didn't put it in the orifice that it's usually inserted into. So, there is that, I suppose."

Nick began to feel that feeling in the pit of his stomach again. And, with another turn of the screw it was accompanied by a combination of ribs cracking and spine-chilling shrieking. Nick watched as the man's kidneys and large intestine began to appear from the wound, popping up and out like popcorn exploding from the kernel, being forced by the expanding metal spoons with each turn of the screw. The veins, nerves, and muscles that once held his organs were being severed by the sharp edges of the spoons. Another turn and his kidneys flew out and struck the henchman on his thigh, freshly staining the already soiled and torn rags he was wearing before dropping to the platform and then bouncing to the ground below. His intestines were already dangling between his open wound and the gravel floor. The reaction from Nick in seeing the man's internal organs fall from his body was to double over down to his knees and he began to dry heave, as nothing solid was left in his stomach to bring up.

"*Hmmm.* It appears the clay isn't working as well as it should," Jeffrey mentioned. He then squatted down to Nick and tapped him on the shoulder, uttering with enthusiasm,

"Oh, did I mention, that cut in his stomach? It's in a way that will cause him to completely tear apart into two pieces when he's stretched to a point that his body can't go any further! Just wait, you'll see! Just wait until you see his reaction!"

"I don't want to see that," Nick whined while waiting for his stomach to contract again, wiping spit from his chin and staring at the ground.

"What? Why?" Jeffrey stood again, appearing confused. "You asked to see this, Nick. You wanted it. Well, now, here it is. Take it all in. Accept it. Embrace it." Jeffrey looked at the victim and motioned, "At least watch when they pull out his finger and toenails with a set of red-hot pincers. That's an added bonus, by the way." Jeffrey pointed, "He didn't start with that. But, like you, he couldn't play by the rules."

Nick heaved again and then looked up at the man being punished. He looked at the tortured man's face. He looked into his eyes, which were staring straight back, although not seeing Nick at all. Regardless, Nick knew that the man was feeling every agonizing horror that was being done to his body. That his every nerve was sharp, his pain receptors were fully intact and his sense of realization was high and alert.

Another turn of the rollers and screws resulted in more cries of anguish erupting through the blood and bile the man was spewing from his mouth, and flesh tore as more bones were broken. The screw was turned again and blood spurted from the wound onto the rags of the executioner, who never flinched, as the man's pancreas appeared from the gaping hole and dropped to the dirt floor. As Nick watched helplessly he knew that the person being tortured hadn't the ability to swoon, pass out, or simply die again. The Boss was making certain of all that. Nick also came to the realization that soon, he himself was to begin to experience something very similar.

Nick lowered his head again to look away. Jeffrey noticed and bent down, and with both hands, he took hold of Nick's head and forced the young man to face the terror.

"Look, Nick! You wanted to see this! You wanted to see it all! So, look at it!" He growled, "It was oh, so easy when you were causing the pain, wasn't it, Nick?! When you walked over those children's bodies after leaving them to die on the floor of that school! But, not so easy when it's one of your own right here in front of you feeling his guts being torn out, now is it?!" Jeffrey violently turned Nick's head to the left, "Look, Nicholas! Look over there!"

Nick saw a third henchman turning away from a cauldron of burning coals. In his leather-gloved hands were a set of long-handled iron pincers, the tips glowing red from the fire they'd just been removed from. Nick struggled as Jeffrey held tight and made his head follow the minion as he ascended the wooden stairs to the platform. Nick was forced to watch as the executioner who had been turning the screw let go of the metal and the huge wingnut bobbed in the air. The demon then took hold of the victim's wrist and held out his hand.

"I don't want to see this!" Nick attempted to close his eyes, but he couldn't. He was unable to force his eyes shut. Something out of his power was in control now.

"Oh, no, Nick! You don't get out of it that easily! You will watch!" Jeffreys's grip on the young man's hair and chin tightened. Nick's hands dug into the soft earth and his muscles tightened as he helplessly fought against Jeffrey's overpowering grip. "Watch what happens when you don't play by the rules! And, I don't mean by the rules down here! I mean by the rules of life itself! Watch what occurs when you make terrible, conscious choices! When you harm others for your own self-gain!"

Jeffrey's anger was seething, and he spat through his clenched teeth as his voice continued to growl, "Watch what happens when heaven throws your ugly carcass away and hell takes you in with open arms!" Jeffrey's face was touching Nick's, "Here is where you will be recognized as you so desperately desired! Here is where you'll be famous!

Here is where your demons will pay close attention to you, as they are with this man!" Jeffrey shook Nick's head, "Here is where you'll get everything that you asked for, and so deserve!" Jeffrey turned Nick's face to his, and he stared straight into Nick's eyes, "And, I promise you, Nicholas, you won't enjoy it! *You won't enjoy any of it!*"

Nick was helpless to resist as Jeffrey turned his head back and forced him to watch as one, two, three fingernails were being plucked by the glowing pincers. He listened to the shrieking as each fingertip was burned by the hot iron, and the blood flowed as the nails were being torn from their roots and tossed to the dirt below. He watched the man's eyes plead with his executioners as they finished with his hand, and they started on his toes. Jeffrey held tight as Nick watched the rollers being turned again and again, and the flesh on the open wound where the metal Pearls of Anguish were sticking from tore open wider across the man's abdomen to the point that the metal device fell out, taking with it more entrails. All of his intestines were now extending and dangling below the rack, and his severed internal organs swimming in the pile of flesh and blood on the ground.

"Please! *Stop!*"

Jeffrey turned Nick's head again and the young man saw fires burning in his host's eyes. He also saw the reflection of himself in Jeffrey's lenses, and he didn't like what he viewed.

"Stop?! *Stop what?!* Stop the pain?! Oh, no, Nicholas! That isn't going to happen! This man's pain will never stop! Just as yours will never cease, either!"

Nick was able to finally force his eyes shut just after the man's body tore in half, his upper body flopping up and over the rack, spewing blood, flesh, bone, and entrails to the stone ceiling above. His lower body's remaining contents striking the executioner on the ground as it flopped down, splashing against his torn, ragged clothing and skin and dripping down to the dirt below his feet.

Nick clenched his eyes tight as the screaming ceased. All

went quiet except that he now heard distant, deep laughter ringing in his ears.

And Jeffrey released his death grip.

◆ ◆ ◆

"What's the matter, Nick? You didn't seem to enjoy that quite as much as I thought you would."

The pair had returned to the corridor. The door disappearing behind them as they wandered away from it. Nick was using the walls to balance himself, as he was a bit unsteady on his feet. Jeffrey's voice had calmed, and his arrogant demeanor returned. "I apologize for the need to be physical with you. However, you were resisting that in which you had so much desired to see."

"I didn't need to see that." Nick wiped his chin again, checking to see if anything remained from his dry heaving. He also wiped Jeffrey's spit from the side of his face.

"Oh, yes you did, Nick. You asked for that. You wanted it. You've been wanting to see that ever since you stepped off the elevator." As Jeffrey said this, another loud, horrible scream came from somewhere ahead of them. "My, my. Busy day today, isn't it?"

Nick stopped, closed his eyes, and placed his back against the cold, dark wall. He let out a heavy sigh, *"Son of a bitch."*

"What's the matter, Nick? Is it the screaming? I hope it isn't getting to you. Just think, it will be even worse when it's your own voice that you hear crying out in pain. At least the one you hear now is someone else's and not yours."

"Is it getting warmer down here?" Nick's eyes were still closed as he wiped his perspiring brow while his other hand fanned his shirt out from his chest.

"I don't believe so. Then again, it could be. I'm quite accustomed to the place, so I really wouldn't know. It feels fine to me. Anyway, come along now. We must carry on."

Jeffrey began walking again and Nick reluctantly pushed

himself away from the wall and followed. Nick increased his stride and took hold of his host's arm, turning him around, panting, "Wait a minute! Stop!"

"What is it, Nick?"

"You said *today*. You said it was a busy day *today*. You didn't correct yourself after. I thought you said time didn't matter? You've been doing this the entire time that we've been walking, contradicting yourself! Well, if time doesn't matter then why the reference to a day?"

"I did? Well, my apologies. I certainly didn't mean to." Jeffrey's sarcasm reflected in the statement.

Nick's anger returned, "Bullshit! You're doing that on purpose! Tell me, does time exist or not down here?! You've been telling me all along that it doesn't! I want to know!"

"Nick, I said I was sorry. I didn't mean to reference that, that does not exist here. It was simply a slip of the tongue. There is no more of the fourth dimension, you only exist in the conscious experience here. Now, come along, our time grows short." Jeffrey flashed a cheesy grin to a visibly annoyed Nick. "Oops, sorry."

◆ ◆ ◆

"Why are we the only ones wandering around here? Aren't there people like me showing up all the time? Why aren't there others being dragged around by someone like you? Aren't people dying every minute?"

Jeffrey frowned and glanced down at his protégé, "Nick, your reference to the pars minuta prima, or minute as you put it, simply doesn't…"

"Shut up about time and answer the question!"

Jeffrey was taken aback, "Well, there's no need to be rude. And, to answer your inquiry, there are others being escorted, and instructed, on the ways of the place. You just simply can't, or should I say, aren't allowed to see them."

Nick's reply was disrespectful and salty, "Oooh, sorry, I forgot. I'm not allowed to make friends down here."

"Well, I'm your friend, Nicholas. Aren't I?"

Nick's eyes rolled, his remark chaffing, "Not as far as I'm concerned."

"Ah, well, such is life. Well, not exactly life…"

"*Shut up.*"

The two walked past many doors without stopping, which was fine with Nick. He felt no need to see any more people being tortured. From each door that they went by he could hear the sounds of complete silence, uncontrollable sobbing, or the ear-piercing screams of someone in their cycle again.

Nick attempted to avoid all of it. "So, do I get to be someone's *pain in the ass* like you someday? Will I be walking newbies around here?"

"Highly unlikely." Jeffrey stopped at the next door and Nick noticed that his host was looking left and right, placing a finger to his chin.

"What's the matter? Forget who's in this room?" The younger man turned to face his host again, remarking quite sarcastically, "Having a momentary lapse of memory, are we? Do we need a map to the stars?"

"No, that's not it, Nick." Jeffrey sighed heavily, peering over the younger lad's head and silently counting doors in the corridor, ending at the one they were standing in front of.

"Then, what now?"

Jeffrey looked down at his friend, an endearing smile crossing his lips, "I'm afraid we've arrived. This one is yours, Nicholas."

Nick's eyes widened, and his head turned to look at *his* door. When he turned back to his host, the corridor wasn't the same as it had been not a micro-moment earlier. And neither was Jeffrey.

Part 9

The Truth is Revealed Along With the Lies

Nicholas stood facing the doorway at the end of the corridor with an arm remaining around his shoulders. They had arrived.

The door staring at Nick was the same as all the others, tall and ominous. The same small window hovered just out of Nick's view, and no chains yet on the door's handle, nor on the large O-ring mounted to the frame. Nick looked the door up and down without moving his head. He saw no number plate, no nameplate, nothing. There was nothing to indicate who the occupant was to be, although he knew it was to be him.

"Well, Nicholas, here we are." The hand of the arm around his neck gave a squeeze to Nick's shoulder. Staring forward, Nick's eyes grew as the voice didn't seem the same as his host had sounded just moments before. The voice was still male, but deeper now. Still with a signature arrogant tone, it simply wasn't Jeffrey's voice. Another squeeze and Nick's eyes glanced at the hand on his shoulder. It was large, larger than Jeffrey's. The grip was strong. The hand had fingernails that were long, and they dug into Nick's flesh through his shirt. It was uncomfortable.

"I hope you'll like the room that I've picked out for you."

Nicholas, who hadn't realized yet that he was trembling, slowly turned his head and looked up. The man holding onto him was still tall, however, taller than Jeffrey had been by an inch, or possibly two. The man, older than Jeffrey had seemed by many years, had distinguishing age lines and dark, thick, and slicked-back hair. He had a neatly trimmed beard and mustache, both black in color, and thick, pointed eyebrows at the base of his prominent forehead. His skin tone was darker than Jeffrey's pale colorization had been. Nick hadn't taken notice yet that the man was wearing a black suit, black tie, and shiny black dress shoes in comparison to Jeffrey's casual dress. His crisp dress shirt also black in color. He was a handsome man and Nick felt immediate intimidation as he stared up through his coke-bottle glasses, and the man's eyes naturally squinted above his own wide smile back down at the young lad.

"Hello, Nicholas."

Nick's voice cracked, but he tried hard to retain his confidence, "Where's Jeffrey?"

The man frowned. "Who? Oh, yes, Jeffrey." His smile widened, "Well, Nicholas, there was no Jeffrey. Oh, certainly the man that you thought was Jeffrey does exist. In his own little space, of course. That's where they all are."

The man spoke calmly, with confidence. Articulate, with arrogance. He turned Nick by his shoulder to face him, towering over his young pupil. "Did you really believe that I'd let him accompany you on your little journey? That I'd allow him the comfort of roaming my halls freely? That I would allow him the pleasure of speaking to another? Or, that I'd allow him the luxury of explaining what this place is? No, no. That's my job. No, Jeffrey is in his place, where he'll remain forever. I would never allow him to roam these halls, no more than I would ever allow you to do so. Only once do you get the opportunity to perform the walk that you and I have accompanied each other on. And that time has now come to a close."

"But I thought…"

"You thought what? No, Nicholas. Jeffrey is in his room suffering along with all the rest. He simply was never here with you. He never saw you. He never spoke to you. He simply doesn't even know that you exist."

"But, I saw him…"

Interrupting with a raise of his prominent brow and cocking of his head, "You saw what? You saw him experience his pain? No, Nicholas. I showed you his pain. All in an effort to help make you understand. Although, it's quite unfortunate that you found amusement in the display, rather than what it was intended to teach you. No, Jeffrey wasn't with you when that occurred. It did occur, that much is for certain. However, he was somewhere else entirely. It's been you and I all along, Nicholas. It always has been."

Nick's eyes intensified, and his voice was low, "Then, you're..?"

"Yes, Nicholas. I am. You did want to meet me, didn't you? In fact, I recall that you demanded to meet me." Lucifer released his grip and presented himself to Nick, still smiling wide. "Well, what do you think, Nicholas? Am I what you expected?" The devil swung his hips side-to-side, "Am I everything you pictured? Am I everything you'd hoped for?" His expression turned to surprise. "No? I'm not?" He smiled again, "Perhaps you expected something else entirely?" As he spoke, Lucifer animated his hands to his own description, "Maybe you thought you'd see reddish skin or glowing eyes? Or, possibly a long snout? Perhaps a pitchfork in my grip. Or, maybe horns extending from my forehead? Ah, cliché, cliché."

Nick attempted to control his trembling that he now noticed, still speaking in a low voice. "I don't know what I expected."

"Of course, you didn't. That's your problem, Nicholas. You didn't want to see reality. You didn't want to live in reality. You don't even know what reality truly is. Only the reality you felt you had control over. Which, of course, you never did. No, no, Nicholas, this is me. And, whether you like it or not doesn't matter a hill of beans." Lucifer raised his thick, black eyebrows, "You see Nicholas, you always felt that you were the only one that mattered. That somehow life owed you something. And, you alone made the decision that you were going to make up the rules."

"What rules..?" Nick's voice was trailing. Every hair on his body was standing straight and the goosebumps had once again appeared on his arms.

Lucifer cocked his head in the opposite direction as he looked down at the young man. "The rules of life, Nicholas. The rules of a decent society. You decided that you would skew them to only suit you, and no other."

The Boss's smile remained and he looked straight into the young man's eyes, "Think of it this way, Nicholas. You were the car that never yielded when entering an expressway full of other vehicles. Even when the passing lane was blocked, you still expected the vehicles in the driving lane to move over for you. You didn't care that the rules indicated that you were the one that was supposed to yield to others. You didn't care that you might cause an accident. In fact, you always wished for one to occur just so you could watch it happen, and then deny that it was you that caused it. You're that person, Nicholas. You always felt that life should move over for you. You were not a team player."

"I'm sorry." The words were quite involuntary. Nick hadn't even realized he'd said them.

The Prince of Darkness reared his head and frowned. "Sorry?" He then shook his head and closed his eyes, "No, no, Nicholas. It's far too late for that. And, you're not really sorry, now are you? You're just saying that for the same reasons all of the others did, and do, in your situation." He sighed, "You all try in some feeble, pathetic attempt to be forgiven. It's so weak and tiresome. Truly, Nick, the time for being sorry was the day you were born." He nodded slightly, "You should have apologized to your parents the moment you were conceived, and even begged them to have used contraception to save them the pain you were going to cause during your existence." Lucifer cocked his head again, raising the eyebrow back up, "But then again, you were a baby, Nicholas. And, babies can't talk, now can they? Still, you were smarter the day you were born than you were the day that you died. Once you were conceived and no longer just a stain in your daddy's underwear, well, everything after that was deliberate. You chose your path and your destiny. You chose how to ruin your life and the lives of others." He pointed and frowned, "Your destiny now being that you belong to me. And, I make up the rules here, Nicholas. Not you." Lucifer perked up as his smile returned, "Now, questions? You must have more questions before our time is done here."

Nick managed a smile and nervously chuckled silently to himself. The devil frowned inquisitively in response as the young man inquired, "Time. You lied to me, didn't you? About time not meaning anything?"

"Of course, I lied to you. I lied about many things. That's what I do, lie and deceive, my dear Nicholas. Did you expect anything less of me?" Lucifer's smile never waned, "But then again, maybe everything wasn't a lie. Maybe none of it was a lie. Who knows, Nicholas? We didn't have a lot of time to get to know each other, so whether I was lying or not, you really don't know. Nor will you ever, I'm afraid. You see, Nicholas, you wasted our time together. You didn't pay attention, nor did you ask intelligent, or relevant questions. Any confusion or questions that remain are no one's fault but your own."

"You lied about being Jeffrey."

The devil nodded and looked up, "Yes, that's true. I did lie about that."

"Did you lie to me about time? Have I really been here for a thousand years?"

"Well, Nicholas. It really doesn't matter, now does it?

Whether we've been walking for an hour, or a thousand years matters not. So, to answer you, possibly it was a lie." He looked sternly at the boy, "But what wasn't an untruth, is the fact that it makes no difference at all. It's all relative to eternity. Time still means nothing down here, whether it exists or not. Now..," Lucifer placed his arm back around Nick's shoulder and faced him to the door, "…we have, in fact, run out of time."

"Wait!" Nick turned back to face his host. "I have more questions."

"Please, Nicholas. You're stalling. And, I have other things to attend to."

Franticly, "No! Wait! Please, tell me, what's behind the door before you open it?!"

A heavy sigh before responding, "I've told you, Nicholas. It's your room. Just your own little space. That's all. Everything to be afraid of, that's what lies on the other side. I can't be any more specific than that."

"Please!"

Lucifer thought for a moment before blinking slowly, "Okay, I'll indulge you one last time." He pointed and scolded, "Although, I shouldn't. This has already been explained to you. It's not my fault that you didn't pay attention."

Nick nodded. He most certainly was stalling.

"So, first, what will occur when it's opened is that you'll see yourself. Like a short film, Nicholas. You'll see what was intended to happen to you when you first arrived, minus the rules you broke, of course. You won't feel the pain, but you'll see it occurring." The devil pointed, "And, please, pay attention. You'll only get to see this once before it occurs for real. It's designed to prepare you. Although, as mentioned, it will be worse when it comes. Rules are rules."

Lucifer placed a hand on each shoulder and directed Nick to face the door again. "And then, you'll wait. Just like all the rest, you'll wait for your turn to arrive. All the while your mental pain and anguish will grow from fear, anticipation, and the unknown to unbearable levels. Plus, I'll throw in a few more things, just to keep your thoughts company. You know, the hunger, thirst, headaches, rash, illness, sexual desires, exhaustion."

Lucifer continued to lecture, both now staring at the door. "Keep in mind, I'm doing these things as a favor to you. It's all designed to help you keep your mind off the physical pain that's pending. You should really thank me for that." Lucifer reached for the door handle, looking Nick in the side of his face. "None of it will be fun, Nicholas. Well, except for me. I'll enjoy watching you suffer quite immensely. It's all for my enjoyment now, and punishment for you. The punishment that you deserved, however, never received during life. I now provide this to you in death."

Just before he reached the handle, Nick stopped him again with his words, *"Wait!"*

The devil sighed another sigh and retracted his hand. "Please, Nicholas. I have other, more important things to deal with. You're now wasting *my time*. And, my time matters. I'm growing weary of you." He faced Nick again, turning the young man just a bit, and raised a finger. Speaking jovially, "Oh, by the way, I so enjoyed your trip back home. I mean, really, I didn't expect anything less. But, to see you make the same poor choices all over again? Classic. I have to thank you for that. It's so rare that someone acts that callous and ridiculous twice in one lifetime. Well, not exactly the correct definition of a lifetime, now is it? I mean, you were dead the second time around, now weren't you?"

Lucifer turned Nick back to the door and moved behind, placing a hand on each of Nick's shoulders, his grip firm. He rested his head near Nick's ears, "But, to act that way all over again? Priceless! I must ask you to participate in my production in the grand theater sometime. I think you'd be very good at it. I think you're a better actor than you may think." He let one hand leave Nick's shoulder to gesture to the door. "Now, shall we?"

Nick answered in a voice filled with fear as he stared straight, "I can't. I'm not ready."

"Whether you're ready or not is of no interest to me, Nicholas. What you want, or are ready for, doesn't matter one bit. Not to mention, there's simply nowhere else to go."

The devil guided Nick to turn around again. The young man now discovered that the corridor had been replaced by solid walls. He was now surrounded on all three sides, plus the door waiting for him. Nick looked to see that they were now standing in a space no larger than six feet square, surrounded not by the same ancient, dark-stained, and burnt woodwork, but rather brickwork on all three sides, and also on the ceiling above. The bricks were faded, the mortar cracked, and the odor of mold surrounded them. Only one solitary candlestick mounted on the wall illuminated the small space.

Nick was trapped, with only one way out, and that was through the door. His claustrophobia was now even more intense and he felt sick to his stomach again. He began to shake more. He could no longer control his body's reactions to where he was. He could no longer control his fear. If he'd still had his genitals, he probably would have soiled himself, and he still felt as if he had.

Lucifer was still leaning into Nick when the lad jumped as the door behind cracked open without being touched by the Boss, which resulted in a thunderous bang. The devil chuckled in his deep, disturbing voice, "I apologize. I didn't mean to startle you."

Nick's eyes shut and his voice cracked, "That's okay."

Lucifer stood straight and faced Nick again with a huge hand on each shoulder, chortling, "It's a new sensation for you, isn't it? Fear. Or, possibly not. Maybe it's just the first time you've ever realized that you are capable of being scared." The devil slid beside Nick and placed his arm around the young man's shoulder again, turning the boy back to face the door. Looking down, "But, what is there to be scared of, Nick? You know what's behind that door, don't you? It's just you. It's just you and what I've chosen for you. I've tried to show you all along. I have attempted to prepare you. So, why be so scared, Nicholas?"

Lucifer cocked his head, "Those children in that school were scared, weren't they? And, the adults too. Wasn't that a sign of weakness to you? Didn't their fear provide you with power? Didn't it amuse you when they cowered and displayed that fear to you? Fear is something you loathed, and power something you coveted, Nicholas. So, why be afraid now?" His host puffed up his massive chest. "Buck up, Nick. Be a man! Take what's coming to you without the display of fear!"

Nick's voice crackled as he stared straight at the wooden door, "I'm not scared."

"Of course, you are! You can't fool me, Nicholas." Lucifer glanced up, having a thought, "Ah, yes! That's it, Nick! It just came to me! A fool! You will play a jester in my theater production. A perfect part for you!" He poked Nick on the shoulder, "You shall dress as a fool, wearing bells on your head and toes, and you shall make me laugh! Well, why not? That's truly what you are, a fool, now isn't it, Nicholas? And, lying about your fear truly makes me laugh! So, you will be a fool in my theater!" He gazed back down at the boy, his smile wide and declaring jovially, "And, when you fail to make me laugh, my dear Nicholas, I shall have your tongue cut out with a straight razor and your eyes removed with a silver spoon! Oh, it will be so amusing!"

Nick's voice was at a whisper, "I don't…"

"…No, no. No need to thank me." Lucifer patted Nick's shoulder, his arrogance ever-continuing, "I revel in such original ideas. I come up with things like this all the time. It's peculiar, though, nobody ever thanks me for my gestures of goodwill." He waved a hand into the air, "Ah, well, que sera sera. It's all much ado about nothing, really." He gestured to the door once again, "Now, if you would, please."

Nick continued to stare. Where the door had cracked

open he felt an even warmer air than what had been encountered thus far wafting out and striking his face, and a low glow from some sort of light source was emitting from the room. Nick's mouth began to open, but he had no words. Nor did he have the ability to enter his room voluntarily. Nick was frozen in place, not allowing his brain to give the command to his limbs to reach out or step forward.

"Nicholas, please. I told you, I have things to do. Maybe your life had no meaning, but my afterlife does. There's a long line waiting and time is precious." Lucifer bent to place his face next to Nick's again, still with a strong hand on each shoulder, "I realize that you're frightened, Nick. The problem that you're facing now is that I simply don't care. I revel in your fear. I bathe in it. And, it's not like you don't deserve what is to come. You do. So please, Nicholas, open the door and step inside the room."

Nick's inability to move remained. The hands on his shoulders felt as if a sack of rocks were weighing him down. The deep voice traveled down Nick's spine and he felt his stomach turning in knots. His body continued to tremble, his legs about to give out. He simply couldn't bring himself to reach out and push the door fully open, knowing well that he wasn't prepared to experience what was on the other side.

Lucifer maintained his tight grip as a frown formed and he spoke directly into Nick's ear, "Having difficulty, Nicholas? Just can't seem to take that first step. No need to fret, simply taking a step won't hurt a bit. No?"

"I can't…"

Lucifer stood back up, tall and straight. "Well then!" A deep, guttural voice uttered the next phrase as he groaned loudly through his clenched teeth, "Allow me to help you!"

The massive door flew open and Lucifer thrust Nick into his room. The young man was hurled into the space. As a result, Nick would never know of the two hoof prints that were left burned into the flesh of his shoulders where he was violently assisted by Satan.

Nick tripped, landing on his feet inside the room and he looked up. His eyes widened at the sight before him. It was exactly what he had been promised. Nicholas gazed in terror at himself. He stared in fear of what was being done to his body. Nick's jaw dropped, however, no sound was he able to emit, and tears immediately filled his eyes and streamed down his cheeks. He saw his own body and soul being tortured in ways he could never have imagined. The horrible images of what he now realized was going to occur to him physically went on for what seemed an eternity, although truly only lasted moments.

Nick and his mirrored image locked eyes with one another, and his tortured soul cried out for help, which he would forever be unable to receive. The sound coming from himself was demonic as the wailing echoed off the tiny room's walls and into Nick's ears. He dropped to a knee, his face contorted and he reached out to the image of what he was enduring, unable to free the agony of the young man that was himself. Nick moaned out loud for the pain his image was enduring as his extended hands shook, trying desperately to reach out to himself. He finally pulled his hands back, tugging at his own clothing as if now beginning to feel what his image was experiencing. He wept uncontrollably while having the ability to do nothing else other than watch.

Satan stood at the doorway, reveling in the comedy he was witnessing. His evil grin was wide, his pointed eyebrows raised high. He never grew tired of these first moments.

Nick barely recognized the deafening screams as his own, and he returned a piercing cry as the warmth of his own blood and flesh flew from the image and struck him in the face. His hands outstretched again, trying to block the image. Nick's terror-stricken eyes stared down at his now crimson-stained shirt. He looked up and cried out once more, a sound that he would come to recognize all too well.

Satan laughed out loud, a howling cackle that echoed

through his corridors. Others who could hear the laughing from the sanctity of their own space, and who weren't in the midst of their own cycles of pain, cowered.

As Lucifer continued his cachinnation, Nick's door slammed shut. And with a wave of Satan's arm the heavy, iron chains were put in place, clanking against the wood, and the padlock rusted shut forever.

And then, silence.

Not a moment later, the Boss regained composure, adjusting his lapel to his massive shoulders. He kissed his hand and patted it on the door, and smiled a smuggest of smiles. He was satisfied that not only did he now own another soul, but that soul would now be receiving the punishment it so deserved. A punishment that would forever never come to an end.

With a nod, he turned to walk away down his corridors to tend to other business.

And Nick's pain began.

finis

Epilogue

Up until this book, my genre of writing had consisted of my memoir, both satirical and serious, and my humor-fiction series. However, I had decided that I wanted to try my hand at the horror genre. I grew up in the era of Stephen King and both being from the same city in Maine, I wanted to give the genre a shot. I am a fan of horror movies, primarily those made in the 70s and 80s, and I'm a huge George Romero fan. Who, coincidentally, was an acquaintance of Stephen King as they worked on several projects together over the years.

The story you just read, although I consider it to be of the horror genre, also purposely served as a social statement on my views about crime and punishment. In that respect, I'd like to take a moment to provide my inspiration for writing the book. A word of warning, though, and if you've ever read my memoir, you'll know that I have strong opinions on the subject matter which certainly influences the story.

As you know the story itself was about a man that had been recently executed for crimes he'd committed and must face the reality of spending eternity in hell for his actions.

It is my honest belief that certain crimes in our society go without the individual, or individuals, receiving the punishments they deserve. Having worked within the criminal justice system as a law enforcement officer and investigator for over twenty years of my professional career, which also included an assignment as a criminal investigator within the state's correctional system, I experienced firsthand what some people are truly like at their core. I also know that there are those who choose to commit crimes that should never be allowed to roam amongst us in our society again. Mind you, it's alright if you don't share this opinion, as most who tend to disagree with me have not witnessed the things that I have throughout my career.

The truth is, again, that there is that certain population that will plan, and commit serious crimes, and this has been a fact throughout our history. There are also those who believe that due to nothing else having worked to correct the issue, with the problem being the criminal mind itself, they feel we should allow these people to continue to be part of our communities and live in our neighborhoods. Also, that those with dangerous criminal tendencies should be treated with some type of compassion. I disagree with both opinions. And, if the people that support these beliefs were to ever experience what I and many others have seen, or what a true 'victim' of a crime has experienced, they would agree that there are those that shouldn't be allowed to roam amongst us freely. The fact remains that you cannot change the true criminal mind no matter how badly you want to, or how you try to force the change.

In my experience, those who believe that we need fewer prisons and more compassion are the ones who believe you can change the thought process of a criminal mind. Unfortunately, the sad truth is that they are fundamentally wrong. There will always remain those who will conspire, plan, and execute criminal activities. This being regardless of what we allow, or attempt to force upon them, in an effort to change their nature.

I also find it quite disturbing when someone protests against proper punishment simply because the crime was committed by an individual within their own circle. They believe that their loved one should receive much less of a punishment or no punishment at all for what they've done. Or, even worse, they deny that a crime has even taken place, to begin with. However, if the crime had been committed by anyone else, they'd want that person punished. This is not only hypocritical, but it's also morally wrong. I have a difficult time in these circumstances. Very often we find that it's these folks that are protesting against punishment and authority, and are only adding to the problem.

I also have an issue with those who coddle the behavior. I always found it disturbing when I'd make an arrest, and the first words out of the perpetrator's mouth was to allow for a telephone to call their 'mommy' or 'daddy' to bail them out of jail simply because they knew it would happen. This only results in the person reciprocating the behavior, and ultimately leads them to commit the same, or worse crimes in the future. And certainly, in these circumstances, we can place part of that blame on the parents.

This also leads to the next thing that I believe; proper punishment begins early. I have seen so many things that are wrong with the juvenile justice system that resulted in not only society but the system itself, creating an adult offender from the juvenile. I understand that we don't like to see our children incarcerated. But, again, I've seen things that most others have not inside of the juvenile detention centers where I served for a period of time as a criminal investigator. From the first major call that I was required to investigate inside the juvenile detention center, I learned that I wasn't dealing with your average youth. I have witnessed many juvenile crimes that have gone unpunished, and it simply leads to that same child believing that what they've done resulted in no significant consequence, which ultimately leads to the child committing a worse offense once they reach adulthood. And, please don't get the wrong idea, the juvenile detention centers I worked within did include proper schooling, counseling, and rehabilitation programs. You can't entirely blame the system if they're offering all that can be offered to make a better person of the child or the adult. In many cases, in holding a conversation with an incarcerated youth I discovered that the detention center was a better environment than what the child had waiting for them at home.

A criminal is derived from all walks of life. You simply can't pick out those with criminal tendencies solely based on how they were raised or whom they spend their time with. It's not something that's determined by wealth or poverty, or by religion. Some have good backgrounds, some do not. You can't predict from birth who will end up indulging in criminal behavior. Individuals from the worst backgrounds become great people, and some who seem to have it all still turn to a life of crime. But, there certainly are signs and signals along the way that should be paid attention to.

I'm also not saying that there aren't other factors that contribute to criminal behavior, such as mental illness. Let's face it, if you choose to commit a heinous crime and either harm or take the life of another, there is certainly a mental illness involved. Having said that, planning criminal actions and being aware of what you're doing doesn't make a person mentally incapable. Nor does it provide an excuse or a defense for the action.

The criminal mind is power-hungry, but it's also most certainly an insane mind. Having said this we must realize that the criminal mind also has the ability to conspire, plan, detail, and execute actions while being fully aware of doing so. This type doesn't deserve to be allowed to avoid proper punishment by claiming a plea of insanity.

Even worse is when we allow the criminal mind to be free in our society with the hopes of receiving treatment for a mental illness while they're allowed to be part of our communities. This is a recipe for disaster and usually results in such. We've all read the stories and watched the news of those who've recommitted their particular crimes while being 'rehabilitated' and integrated within our communities. The truth is, that we need to have penal institutions for those with serious criminal tendencies to place them outside of the boundaries of society so that both populations can be safe and they can be treated in a proper, controlled setting.

It's not fair to force communities to be required to deal directly with a person who has committed a serious, or series, of crimes. We as a normal society have the right to live without being in constant fear of what someone else might do to us when we least expect it. We already live in that fear every day when we to go work, school, or even out shopping, not knowing who may seek to cause us harm. By adding the element of someone who's already proven to be a danger to society isn't fair to everyone else who abides by laws and has the right to feel safe. This is what causes the average person to take up arms and, at times, take the law into their own hands.

This also makes the job of those who chose the profession of protecting and serving much more dangerous and restrictive. Many times it's the people that are complaining that, "We didn't do enough to prevent it," are the same ones that don't want to allow the proper punishment to deter the individuals from ever doing it again. This makes little sense to me and seems to have caused us to turn around and go entirely in the wrong direction. When the average citizen is forced to protect their family and property, at times through the use of violence, because the system won't properly punish the person who is committing the crime, then we've truly lost our focus on what the criminal justice system was designed to do. Not to mention, we continue to lay the blame on law enforcement and continue to restrict what they are allowed to do to protect the public from the offenders.

I'm also not a fan of making prisons into some type of second home for the individuals, either. If we don't make it uncomfortable for those who've been incarcerated, what message are we sending them back out onto the streets with? When did the term "punishment" become simply defined as re-housing the individual for the weekend stay? I've experienced those who believed their living environment inside prison was far better than their natural environment on the outside. All this serves to prove to the perpetrator is that it wasn't so bad to commit their crimes. Serving their time comfortably simply provides these people with an additional excuse to re-commit once they've been released because being on the inside just wasn't that bad.

I'm a believer that prison should not only be a place of voluntary rehabilitation, but the stay should include a strict regimen to be followed, not for the prisoners themselves to control. Mandatory working and educational programs, no overcrowded recreation yards that encourage gang behavior, and no contact visits of any kind. Luxuries should be envied, not provided, and something to look forward to once they are released if that day should even ever arrive for them. And, let's face it, for those who are imprisoned for life, there's a good reason for it. Let's not make it out to be a summer camp with cake, ice cream, and a bedtime story. Time in prison should not be simple. It should be mundane at best, it should provide rehabilitation and educational opportunities and should serve to teach a lesson on the price of freedom without being torturous.

Again, prisons should not be a place where the prisoners themselves are in control of the facility. As mentioned, I worked as a criminal investigator for the state's Department of Corrections. Now, think about this concept for a moment; being required to have law officers whose sole purpose is to investigate crimes that are taking place inside penal institutions. In fact, I'm going to wager that anyone reading this didn't realize that these types of officers even existed. And, we're not talking about petty crimes taking place, we're talking about serious crimes that involved physical assaults, sexual assaults, murder, extortion, and drug crimes. What type of justice system punishment is taking place when inmates are committing crimes on the inside that are just as serious, if not more, than what they were committing on the outside? What type of rehabilitation is this? And, I'm being honest when I say that many of my best drug cases were generated inside correctional institutions, not on the streets. How is it that a person can commit the same types of crimes while serving time inside prison? This is not the behavior of someone who is rehabilitating themselves and preparing to re-enter our communities. This is the behavior of those who don't care, and also don't deserve anything other than the punishment of incarceration itself.

The argument that many in our current society repeatedly bring up is that those with criminal tendencies require rehabilitation. That those who can be rehabilitated should be. I completely agree. However, I also realize two things about this concept. First; that forced rehabilitation doesn't work, and never has. Second; some simply cannot be, nor are they willing to be rehabilitated. Once we as a society finally realize these two things maybe we can begin to make a plan and cause a positive change.

As you can well imagine, I'm a fan of capital punishment. I'm also a believer that once a person has made the choice to rob another of their right to live a safe life and choose to commit a crime against another, then they give up their basic human rights. I cannot defend the rights of those who violate the safety of others by committing certain crimes, such as murder, sexual assault, child abuse or neglect, certain drug crimes, or even crimes that involve taking personal belongings from others who have worked hard for what they have. Once a crime has been committed, the person or persons involved have chosen to turn their back on society's basic rules, and, in turn, have given up their basic rights. Additionally, on the subject of capital punishment, I believe that if you take something from someone, including their life, then you owe that debt to society. My question is why should someone that has recklessly taken a life away from another have the ability to live out their own at society's expense?

There are also those that believe capital punishment to be cruel. I would argue that it's no less cruel than what the person inflicted on their victims through their actions. In fact, capital punishment is far more humane than what all those who've received the sentence have done to their victims. So, in my opinion, capital punishment should continue as they are in some states today. Other states that never had, or have abolished capital punishment, should reevaluate that decision entirely.

So, to digress, the story that you read in a significant way reflected my ideology on how people who possess a criminal mind and act on those impulses, should be dealt with when it's time for their final judgment. Now, don't get me wrong, this was not meant to be a book about religion even though it dealt with the concept of heaven and hell. My religious beliefs, if any, were not intended to overshadow the story whatsoever. It's simply what it's intended to be, a horror story written with the inspiration behind it.

The second reason for writing a book of the horror genre, and a simpler reason, is the fact that I was born on Halloween. I've always been interested in the history of the Day of the Dead, including the modern traditions that are associated with the holiday. The ghosts, witches, and goblins that children dress up as on that scary evening as they beg for treats or threaten a trick are something I've long enjoyed and participated in as a child. And, as mentioned, in my youth and adulthood I've continued to enjoy a good horror story.

I hope you enjoyed the book and didn't allow my inspiration for writing it to overshadow your opinions now that you've read it. As I've always said, everyone's entitled to their opinion, even if yours isn't the same as mine.

ABOUT THE AUTHOR

David Wilson is a native of Maine, born in Bangor in the late 1960s. Books written include his satirical memoir, *Peanut Butter Memoirs*, and his Maine humor-fiction series, *Two Seasons* and *Ma's Diner*.

David's career spanned many years in public safety including uniformed street patrol, investigations, and agent for the state's drug enforcement agency. David's years living in rural Maine, along with his career, are often found to be inspirations for his books.

David now lives in central Maine along with his wife and their several pets. He continues to enjoy such hobbies as fishing and canoeing the lakes and streams surrounding their home, as well as his writings and artwork.